Forgotten Hills

RENEE LAKE

FORGOTTEN HILLS
Copyright © 2020 by Renee Lake

ISBN: 978-1-68046-893-9

Published by Satin Romance
An Imprint of Melange Books, LLC
White Bear Lake, MN 55110
www.satinromance.com

Published in the United States of America.

Cover Design by Caroline Andrus

To my daughters Tatiana and Ophelia. This is the type of sister relationship I hope you have and the type of adventures (though less scary).

To sisters everywhere.
May you love, support and cherish one another.

ONE

Oregon 1998

Not every little girl spent her summers in a cemetery, winding through old weather-worn headstones. Some headstones were so old you couldn't read the writing anymore. Many were bleached by the sun, others covered in the lichen that grew on anything that stood still.

The three sisters loved to run in the deep green grass that always seemed to be up to their ankles and took afternoon catnaps among vines and under the sweeping boughs of old willow trees. They played hide and seek around the carcasses of trees that died years ago and were never cleared away.

Forgotten Hills Cemetery always smelled like a combination of fresh dirt, cut grass and the delicious scent that rain hitting hot pavement makes.

An eight-foot stone wall surrounded the tiny cemetery, so it was a little girl's ultimate private playground, free from anyone gawking, trying to make conversation or scolding.

"I wish we could live here always," Morana said.

Thana glanced at her youngest sister. They were lying side by side in their favorite spot, the cemetery's center between two weeping angels that time had eroded so badly their faces were blurs of marble.

This special spot was a little higher elevation than everything else. They liked it because they could see everything, but no one could see them. Elder, their pet name for a large dead and formidable oak tree, shaded the angels and space between.

The path from the gate to their secret spot was a big swirl leading right up to the hill where they sat, a flat packed dirt line sweeping around the entire place curling toward them like a snail's shell.

"It wouldn't be fun anymore," Dolores said. She was on her stomach, head cradled in her arms, basking in the end of summer's warmth.

Thana watched as the faint breeze stirred her straw-colored hair. Everyone said that at twelve she was becoming quite the beauty. You know, if not for *it*.

"Lola's right. Just enjoy the days we have left. Mama and Papa will be here in a week to take us home," Thana said. She was sitting, head resting against the slab of rough marble that made a perch for the largest angel

"I wonder what the schools here are like? I bet they aren't full of kids who hate you." Morana sighed and closed vivid blue eyes. She was lying next to Lola, on her back, knees bent.

"Kids at home don't hate you," Thana said. She was worried. Morana was eight and already being bullied at school for something that wasn't her fault, let alone anyone's business.

"You guys are lucky," Morana said.

Lola sat up and moved behind their sister, "Enough of that, c'mon, I'll braid your hair."

Morana reluctantly agreed and slowly moved into a better position so Lola could work on her overly long auburn hair.

Lola's powder blue eyes met Thana's across their little sister's head. They had discussed all summer whether to tell their parents about Morana being bullied. They were leaning toward telling their aunt instead.

"Sing to me, Lola?" Morana asked, eyes still closed, swaying, just a little, but not enough to disturb the braid making.

"Alright, but only to cheer you up," Lola agreed.

Thana closed her eyes again and tried to relax. Every summer she and her sisters spent two and a half months with their aunt. It was a magical time. Thana's first memory was sitting on her aunt's lap, only three years old, being told she would soon have a new sister.

Summers were two and a half months of late nights, languid mornings and eccentric means of fun.

Their mom was an archeologist and their dad a surgeon. They shared a love of history and every summer went on trips to dry, dusty, hot places while Thana and her sisters stayed in Hill City, Oregon.

Honestly, it was better this way. Mom and Dad were great, but their trips sounded so boring!

Their aunt ran and owned Forgotten Hills Mortuary and Cemetery, though the cemetery part hadn't had a burial in more than a decade, due to space issues. It took a bit to get used to the idea of living around dead people, but Thana and her sisters now enjoyed their summers more than anything else.

Besides, the house didn't look like how she imagined a funeral home. Just outdated and misshapen.

A puff of grayish smoke caught her eye, she followed it

knowing exactly where it came from. On the other side of the house where the cemetery ended and the woods began, there was another building. A crematory. The road up to the house circled around to that side making it easier to access.

Thana didn't go over there much, it was an ugly place. A square brick room that didn't match the loveliness of Forgotten Hills. A smokestack sat on top and occasionally, smoke and even rarer flame, would come out of it.

She'd never been inside and didn't want to. She knew bodies went in whole and came out ash. She was only glad that some miracle of science made it so the smoke didn't smell.

Thana listened as Lola's sweet voice sang softly about love and roses, it was the only song they knew in Spanish. Morana hummed with her. Opening her eyes, she let her gaze drift to the house, wondering when their aunt would call them for dinner. She looked up, and in between the gnarled oak branches, she could see the sun, playing peekaboo. She estimated it was around supper time, if not earlier. One of their aunt's rules was dinner around the table, every night.

The mortuary for Forgotten Hills looked like it came straight from the pages of a villain's handbook, like an evil witch would step out onto the large porch amidst the moss and vines to offer poisoned fruit or forbidden candy.

It was a large, house-like structure. Thana and her sisters rarely went to the front of the house where the chapel was and where the office and funeral rooms were. Instead, they used a back staircase next to the kitchen and dining room that wound up to the second floor and the family rooms.

Thana could see the second floor's dirty glass windows from where she sat. From the outside, a tower-like appendage hid the window to her aunt's bedroom. The other windows on this side were the living room and library. The three bedrooms they slept in faced the driveway in the front and the woods to the east.

Thana wished her room looked out on the beautiful graveyard instead of the gravel and dust filled driveway that led to a parking lot riddled with potholes and faded parking lines.

A proper gate to the cemetery was placed near the road as well. The gate was tall, iron, with a padlock that helped keep out trespassers. A one-car dirt road led to a small circle so cars could come into the sacred space, but not very far. If you wanted to experience everything Forgotten Hills had to offer you had to get out and hoof it.

Thana and her sisters never used this opening. The wall that surrounded the cemetery enclosed the back of the mortuary. Thana only had to step out the back door to enter the dead playground.

There were bushes of deep green placed just so visitors didn't realize a small path to the house was there. From their special spot, Thana could see the back door, a simple piece of brown wood with a bronze handle, covered by a mesh screen.

Lola finished singing and braiding around the same time.

"I wish Mama would teach us another song," Morana said, sighing.

"She says it's the only one her mother sang her. She barely remembered what the lyrics meant," Lola reminded her, dotting the braid with tiny white flowers.

"It'd be cool to speak a second language," Morana said.

"Sure, but then you have to have a mom who still actively speaks it and a dad who doesn't get twitchy when she does," Thana said. She hated this particular conversation.

"Aunt Lorelei could teach us," Lola suggested, ducking her head as she earned a glare from her big sister.

"There's no point in asking, end of subject." Thana

crossed her arms over her chest and gave them her best this-discussion-is-over stare.

"There, you look beautiful, as always," Lola said, tucking a stray strand behind their sister's ear and effectively changing the subject.

"I wish I could wear it like this for always," Morana said.

"Why can't you?" Thana asked. Morana did look cute. Just like a tiny version of their mother, especially now that her skin had darkened even more with the sun's attention. All three girls had skin the color of almonds, reflective of their Hispanic heritage.

"*It* shows too much," was all her sister would say.

She was right, the braid did show *it* off. Thana wished Morana didn't care. Morana had a large blood red birthmark that crept up her neck feathering over the right side of her chin and curving around her right eye.

Thana and Lola shared this birthmark, but in different and less noticeable places. Lola's spread from the middle of her left calf and covered the back of her leg. Thana's right arm had it from her inner wrist to elbow.

At fifteen, Thana understood that people, in general, sucked. She tried to impress that upon her younger sisters on a regular basis. Kids in their hometown sucked because they treated them like plague victims. Grown-ups in their hometown sucked because they thought the girls' parents were strange and their parents sucked because they failed to notice anything outside of their work.

There were only two people, outside of her sisters, that didn't suck. One was her aunt.

"Aunt Lorelei is calling us for dinner!" Morana jumped up, excited. Dinner with their aunt was always unique. She was a great cook and loved to try different recipes. Last night it was homemade sushi, the night before a curry dish and last week they ate fancy desserts every night, but one. Sometimes she asked for help and taught them to cook, sometimes she kept it as a surprise.

Thana glanced toward the funeral home and saw their aunt standing at the door to the house, she was smiling and waving. Thana heard her husky voice calling their names. Thana looked like her aunt in many ways. Both were a bit on the chubby side with more black curly hair than was manageable and large periwinkle blue eyes surrounded by thick lashes.

Lorelei had nut-brown skin and was six foot tall. Normally she wore skirt suits in vibrant colors, but during her off hours, she favored loose cotton dresses covered by colorful pinafores that she made herself. Thana hoped she could be as cool when she grew up.

Lola stood, helping Morana up and dusting grass and dirt from their cut off shorts and old t-shirts.

"Where's the picnic basket?" Morana asked, looking around. They always took lunch out into the cemetery so they didn't bother Lorelei when she was busy in the basement with the creepier aspects of her job. Thana didn't mind the dead, they played on top of them all day. Her sisters, though, wanted nothing to do with the dead people stored in the basement.

"I think we left it near the Ring. I'll go get it," Thana volunteered, heart rate increasing ever so slightly.

The Ring was their name for a group of headstones in the very western corner placed in a circle. The names were worn and chipped, but the dates were all the same: September 17th, 1895. It was the only place in all of Forgotten Hills that gave Thana a bit of fear, but even so, it was their favorite spot for lunch. It was away from view from any visitors, very quiet and got the most sunlight of any spot in the cemetery.

It was special to Thana for another reason as well. As her sisters gathered up their other outdoor supplies, she went off in search for the basket.

They never took the main paths. Thana and her sisters had

their own ways to get around. She weaved around headstones and under tree branches, slipped behind bushes and over rocks. Happiness surged through her, tinted with sadness that their summer was coming to an end.

Finally, she spotted the Ring and their basket sitting in the middle of it. As she entered the circle a chill went up her spine and not the normal kind. Not like when the faint breeze dries sweat on your back. The kind laced with the knowledge you are not alone, and something is watching you.

"You'd forget your head if it wasn't attached," a voice from above her said.

Startled, but no longer scared, she looked at the top of the wall nearest her. Sitting on the stone, legs dangling, was a scrawny boy about her age.

"What are you talking about?" Thana asked. She put her hands into the pockets of her jean shorts and stared down at her dirt covered feet, smiling.

"You leave this here a few times a week," he told her.

"It's a pain to lug around the whole cemetery," she explained, looking at him.

His hair was gray, bordering on silver and his eyes were the palest seafoam green. He was the whitest white boy she'd ever laid eyes on, including her father.

"Or you just want to see me," he joked.

Draven—what kind of name was that, really?—never came any closer than the wall, but she'd known him for years. They'd met when she was five. He was the only other child she ever had contact with while in Hill City. A few times a week they'd meet and talk, laugh and joke. He never told her where he lived or anything about his family, but she'd poured out her life history to him.

Once she accused him of dying his hair and he simply laughed, neither confirming or denying it. Whenever she talked about him meeting other people, he became shy and nervous.

She'd wanted to share him with her sisters or to ask her aunt about him, but he'd requested one thing from her these past ten years. That she did not tell anyone about him.

Thana assumed he came from an abusive home. She had a friend like him in school once, private and shy of strangers. Her friend had been sent to live with grandparents when it was found out her dad was hurting her.

Thana didn't want to get him in trouble but hoped after all these years he would at least trust her with the truth.

"My parents will be here by week's end," she told him. He looked thoughtful for a minute.

"Before September, as usual."

"Yeah, gotta be home before school starts." Her heart was thudding in her chest, over the past two summers something had changed when she looked at Draven. She didn't just see her best friend, but a boy, an attractive boy.

"How's Morana?"

"Still being bullied." Thana wondered if he thought she was pretty and if he'd ever come down off the wall so she could touch him.

"Teach her the trick I taught you."

Two years before he'd taught her a way to stand and speak so people would leave her alone, she'd taught Lola, it was time to teach Morana too.

"I'm trying, but she's sensitive."

"Cause it's on her face?"

She nodded. "I just wish my parents paid more attention."

"Talk to your aunt, she understands."

"I doubt it, Lorelei is awesome. She's never felt like that."

"Yes, she has, she grew up with it, too."

Shock coursed through Thana's system. Her aunt had the

same birthmark? Did that mean her mother did too? How come she'd never shown her?

"How do you know that? Did your parents tell you?" she asked, squinting up at him. He wasn't paying attention to her, and his eyes had a faraway look as he stared into the cemetery toward the house.

Then he did something so unexpected she took a giant step back. He jumped off the wall.

"What the hell?" He was taller than she'd imagined, towering over her by a foot. He was so much more handsome up close, his lips curving, and eyes tilted at the edges.

"I'm sorry, Thana," he said, stepping closer to her.

"Sorry for what?" she asked, a little breathless.

His hands feathered up her bare arms, leaving goosebumps in his wake. The palms of his hands and pads of his fingers soft and warm.

"This," he said and then he kissed her. Her very first kiss. Warm, with light pressure. He tasted like the cemetery smelled. She wrapped her arms around his thin waist. He shuddered under her touch and the kiss ended. He stared into her eyes for a second and quickly pulled away.

Before she could understand what had just happened, he scrambled up the wall and perched there, looking wary.

Suddenly Lorelei was coming through the bushes, eyes hard as she stared at Draven, mouth set in a firm line.

Great, had it been that long? Was she in trouble for being late to dinner? Had Lorelei seen them kissing? It wasn't like her aunt to be cross.

"I had a feeling I'd find you here," her aunt said, voice dark with anger.

Thana began to speak and realized she wasn't being spoken to, Draven was.

"I told you to stay away during the summers," Lorelei snapped at him.

Thana was confused, how could she be mean to a kid?

"It's okay, Aunt, I know him, he's my friend." Thana touched her arm.

Lorelei looked down at her for a moment and her eyes softened and filled with sadness, "It's not your fault, Querida."

She looked back at Draven who had a stormy and serious expression on his boyish features, "How long? What have you said to her?"

"Ten years and nothing of significance," he answered.

That hurt Thana's feelings, nothing they had talked about was significant? What was going on?

"Did you touch her?" Lorelei asked.

"No." His eyes didn't leave Thana's face as he lied.

Lorelei looked to her niece. Thana knew a blush was spreading, cherry red, over her neck and face.

"Hmmm," she said. It was obvious she didn't believe him.

"I have not done anything to harm her," Draven spoke it like a promise.

"I must end this now," Lorelei sighed, fists clenched at her sides.

"I know," Draven said. He looked at Thana, eyes downcast. "I have enjoyed spending time with you, Thana. I have looked forward to seeing you over the summers. You are very special to me, please believe that."

"What's going on, Draven?" Thana felt fear curl in her belly. He was special to her too. She didn't like the confusion coursing through her.

"Go, now!" Lorelei demanded. Thana watched as Draven turned and disappeared over the wall. She felt a heaviness in her chest, as if tears were living behind her eyes.

Lorelei took hold of her shoulders and leaned down to look Thana in the eyes. "Querida, speak truly, do you know who that was?"

"Draven," Thana answered, shakily.

"That's it? He didn't say anything else, didn't touch you?"

"No, he said his name was Draven...I...I don't know much about him. He's my friend."

Lorelei gripped her harder. "He is not that. You are never to speak to him again, understand?"

Thana nodded her head, tears seeping from under her eyelids, running down her cheek. Her aunt hugged her, smelling of menthol and pine.

"Come on, Querida, let's go have dinner." Lorelei picked up the basket and led the way back to the house.

It was the last summer they spent at Forgotten Hills.

TWO

Oregon, 20 years later

THANA COULD ONLY STARE AT THE HOUSE. SHE HAD HER phone clasped in one hand, still hot from being overworked by the GPS, and the envelope containing keys in the other. The metal keys were digging into her palm through the paper.

Forgotten Hills was exactly as she remembered it, Hill City too. Like time froze these last twenty years. The misshapen funeral home's ethereal beauty and all its lumpy parts was a nerve-racking and welcoming sight.

The cemetery loomed to the right side and behind the house. Slowly she walked over to the gate, hands gripping the cool iron she peered through, feeling fifteen again. Everything was green, and everything was the same, though older and possibly a bit more overgrown.

"Was the house always green?" Morana asked from behind her.

"Kind of," Thana said, looking back at the house. It was a

rather odd mix of turquoise and sea green with dark brown borders.

"It looks the same. I thought it would be smaller, but it's not," Morana said, stepping closer to her sister.

"Well, let's go inside, this is home now." Thana motioned toward the large stairs that led up to a porch that was big enough for a small dinner party.

The front door was wide, deep brown and made from solid wood, the locks ornate and brass. Thana ripped open the envelope. Taking out the key, she shoved it into the lock, and it clicked open.

"I don't remember Lorelei using a key, this door was always open," Morana commented.

"Probably why the lock is stiff, so put that on the list of things to do." Thana pushed the door open and they were greeted by warm and sweet-smelling air.

They stepped through the doorway and looked upon a familiar sight, the reception room with its hardwood floors, giant windows covered in forest and cream curtains and an odd collection of chairs for a family to wait in. There were paintings of horses on the walls Lorelei had painted herself. A desk sat in one corner with a computer, lamp and a stack of documents. Thana hoped Lorelei hadn't left them a bunch of bills in her will as well.

"Well, let's see if her lawyer was right and the caretaker got it ready for us," Thana said. Taking a deep breath, she flipped a switch by the door and the room was illuminated with soft overhead lights.

Morana let out the breath she'd been holding. "That's good, we won't have to worry about the utilities." She walked over to the desk and ran her finger over the wood. "No dust, the caretaker did a good job."

Lorelei fell five years ago, coming down the back staircase. She'd gone to a rehab facility and from there an assisted living center. She died last month. When they got the call, Thana couldn't believe it. In her mind's eye, Lorelei was still spry and beautiful. Her mom gently reminded her that Lorelei was her older sister, after all.

"Sixty-five isn't old," Thana said to no one in particular.

"It is when you break a hip and suffer a brain aneurysm," Morana commented.

"I can't believe she left the house and the cemetery to us," Thana said. It wasn't the first or the second time the sentence had left her mouth.

"It's primarily yours, you're the actual mortician." Morana went to the door next to the desk and opened it and found an office.

"It couldn't have come at a better time. When will Lola be here?" Thana ducked down one dim hallway that sprouted off the reception room; a chapel with a connected family room, visitation room, and a bathroom. She'd do a more detailed walkthrough later. Lorelei had also left them some money. They'd agreed to use it and spruce the place up. She was pleasantly surprised how warm and inviting, albeit eccentric, the place was. It didn't look like it needed much work.

Another closed door on the left side led down a shaded hall with no windows. The air was stale in the hallway.

"You go first," Morana said, she grinned and gave her sister a push.

"Coward. There are no ghosts in a mortuary." These words aside, Thana felt around for another light switch and was immensely glad when the light came on. The hall was hardwood with pale green paint and the girls were delighted when it opened into a very airy room with several small windows that looked out onto the cemetery. Each window had a lacy white curtain and a plant on the sill.

"I'll have to give that caretaker a bonus."

"Probably some sweet old woman who was friends with our aunt," Morana said. She was inspecting the kitchen.

Morana was still the smallest sister. She had a very slim figure and barely topped five foot one. Her auburn hair was cut short in a pixie cut and now a pair of black-rimmed glasses sat on her nose. Her birthmark was ever present on her face today. When she worked with the public, she used a very expensive and powerful concealer foundation combo to cover it.

Morana checked every single detail, including turning on the faucet over the deep kitchen sink to check for water pressure.

"How's the setup?" Thana didn't know anything about kitchens. This one was all white and stainless steel. It was a decent size and the appliances were newer than she remembered.

"It works, may need to make a few purchases, some adjustments, but it will do nicely." Morana finished speaking, wiping her hands dry on her jeans. "I think Lorelei must have renovated a bit before her fall. We got lucky."

Morana was a chef. She owned a small bakery in Portland, and she did quite well at it. Her current fascination was filling out as many applications as she could to get on a food network show. She was planning to cater the party they threw for the reopening.

She already had a notebook filled with ideas; brie and bacon spinach dip, smoked salmon quiche, a three-tiered rum raisin coffin shaped cake and frosted sugar cookie headstones. Just to name a few.

"You sure you don't need to get home?" Thana asked, walking to the fridge and opening it. The emptiness disappointed her, but what had she expected, really?

"No, no… Trixie said she could manage for a month or two while I helped you get things settled. She understands."

Trixie, or Beatrice, was Morana's wife and business partner. They'd been married for four years.

The door to the cemetery was the same, but for the first time, ever Thana noticed it was locked. Though she guessed it made sense. Her aunt hadn't lived here for five years.

The small alcove that held the dining room and back stairs was next to the kitchen. Morana rushed toward the pantry door and opened it. A few sad cans of green beans were the only thing on the shelves.

Next to the pantry was an even tinier laundry room.

"This space isn't utilized very well," Morana said, "And that table has to go."

Thana made a mental note to buy a new table and chairs and went upstairs.

"Should Lola have a room facing the road or the woods?"

"The road because the sun rises that way," Thana said. The house smelled like their aunt. It smelled of clean dirt, pine, and menthol. She had no idea how it had retained the same scent all these years, but it had. It was a comfort, and they needed it.

The upstairs hadn't changed. Small living room, bathroom, three bedrooms, and a library.

"Let's give her mom's old room," Thana said.

Forgotten Hills hadn't just been Lorelei 's. Their mother had grown up here too. Their mother's family owned the property since pioneer days.

"Why doesn't mom ever talk about living here? All I remember is how much fun we used to have." Morana sat down on the deep brown couch, she sank into it and made a noise of contentment.

"You know mom, if the past isn't something she can dig up and write a paper on, she doesn't talk about it. I always got the impression she was embarrassed coming from such a small town. Grandma and Grandpa Burke weren't very nice about her roots," Thana said.

Their paternal grandparents were white and rich, they hadn't been thrilled with their parent's match. The chubby Hispanic girl wasn't who they pictured their perfect son marrying. But their father loved their mother more than anything in the world and couldn't be persuaded against marrying her. Their mom had spent decades trying to live up to their expectations.

"Grandma and Grandpa Burke are the worst," Morana said, snorting. On this, they could agree.

The living room's furniture was a jumble of mismatched pieces from ornate end tables, DIY bookshelves, lazy boys covered with home crocheted afghans and what seemed to be a thrift store coffee table. The carpet was worn and beige.

"Hope the bedrooms are in better condition, we are for sure going to do some shopping."

Morana perked up at this. "Ikea?"

Thana nodded her consent. Checking her phone, she got another surprise, wi-fi!

"Oh, Thana, look." Morana sat forward, eyes focusing on the wall next to the large TV. Thana looked and her chest hurt for a moment, heart thudding. On the wall were multiple 5x7s of her and her sisters from birth to their college graduations. There was an 8x10 from Morana and Trixie's wedding day as well as one from Lola's.

"I didn't think she cared anymore, not after she told us we couldn't come back."

"Obviously, there was a reason she said that and not for lack of affection."

Morana walked over and grabbed Lola's wedding picture from the wall.

"Stash that someplace. I don't want to see it," Thana said.

Morana grinned. "Should we burn it?"

"No, Lola might want it, someday."

Morana nodded and went to the linen closet, burying the offending picture under the old ratty swim towels.

"What now?" Morana asked, "Should we tackle the bedrooms? Call to have an inspector come out? Deal with the basement and see if you need a complete overhaul? Get online and find a contractor?"

"I think we should go back into town and buy some groceries."

THREE

THANA SAW DRAVEN TWICE MORE AFTER HER AUNT TOLD HER she could never see him again. The last time was unexpected, to say the least. In fact, she was never sure he was really there or if it was all a dream.

When she graduated school with a Bachelor's Degree in Mortuary Sciences, her parents threw a party in San Francisco for her. She already had an internship lined up and was happy, as happy as she had been at Forgotten Hills.

Of course, her parents didn't come to the celebration, but they paid for everything. Both her sisters and two of her closest friends were invited. They had a spa day, ate a fancy dinner and saw a show.

Upon getting back to the hotel, the five of them drank copious amounts of alcohol until 3 a.m. Everyone stumbled to bed leaving Thana alone. Her sisters and friends were sharing rooms, but as the girl of the hour, as her father said, she had a suite to herself.

A knock at the door.

Very drunk and wearing a pair of red boy-cut underwear and a matching tank top, Thana opened the door. In hindsight, a very stupid act. She was rolling on the liquid high in her stomach; flooding her veins was the emotional rush of succeeding in a dream years in the making.

Opening the door revealed a surprise she couldn't have conjured in her wildest dreams.

"Draven?" She only remembered he looked like he always had, just grown up and taller, broader.

"Thana, congratulations," he said, eyes raking over her form.

"Come in!" She sang out, flinging the door open wide and yanking him inside.

The door slammed, and she jolted from the noise and giggled.

"Thana," he said, but she wasn't paying attention, the vodka in her system making all the moves. She pushed herself against him, mouth on his throat she made a purring noise and it was the last clear memory she had.

She recalled his arms winding around her, hands splaying over every inch of exposed skin.

"I didn't come here for this," he said, mouth on her collarbone.

"We don't have to do this if you don't want to," she said, feeling hot breath on her breast. "Just fuck me already, Draven." Her lips were on his, their tongues intertwined. She tasted like booze and cranberry, he tasted like…home.

When she looked at those hazy memories, she remembered him taking her on the floor, again in the bed and once more as they showered together. She recalled heat, the prickly rug, struggling with a condom wrapper, shrieking when the water was just a little too cold and pleasure so intense it was painful.

She woke the next morning and he was gone, aside from a messy bed there was no evidence he'd been there at all, she wasn't even sore. Hungover, she cried until it was time to meet her companions for breakfast.

———

"This is your new future, and things will be different here."

Thana stood on the top stair, looking down to the complete darkness that led into the basement. She'd rarely been down in the basement since it had been off-limits when she was little. She'd never seen bodies come or go either, so it was a mystery how to even get them down into the preparation rooms. The mortuary she'd worked in the past six years was all one level and three times as big as Forgotten Hills.

She awoke this morning in her aunt's old room. She'd need to replace the bed, but aside from adding her own personal effects, she wasn't going to change a thing. It just felt right to keep her aunt's eclectic art and jewel-toned furniture. She'd wound her long black hair into a bun at the top of her head, gotten quickly dressed and skipped breakfast. She had to get down into the basement and see what the damage was.

Finding the light switch, she turned it on and was happy when bright florescent light filled the stairwell and lit up the basement's dark corners. Only seven steps led downstairs and she smelled the familiar chemical scents that came with a mortician's trade.

Surprisingly there was only one room. It was large and had concrete floors with drains. The walls weren't painted, there was nothing of her aunt's cheer in this room. The room spanned the entire house's length. It was very cold. It looked as if her aunt put some money into keeping the prep room updated. The entire space seemed to be OSHA compliant and properly ventilated. There were multiple biohazard containers for various waste along one whole wall. She'd still need an inspector to come out, but everything looked in great shape.

The tension in her shoulders released as she realized the space was perfect and she wasn't going to have to spend thousands of dollars on renovation, equipment and getting up to code.

A locker for valuables sat in one corner, a shelf with drawers marked: cleaning products, cosmetics, wrist/toe tags sat next to it. There was a single stretcher resting in between two doors at the far end. The only hint of her aunt was folded on the stretcher, a gray and blue hand sewn quilt to cover bodies.

Two embalming tables were in the middle as well as a state-of-the-art Water Control Unit and the embalming machine.

The prep room looked like the one she'd left only four months before. Regret shivered through her as she thought about her last job. What had been a dream position in Virginia had become a nightmare.

"Don't think about it," she told herself. She hadn't done anything wrong and now she had a new future to look forward to.

Thana walked to a long counter at the room's front. The counter was stainless steel and had drawers and shelves filled with tools of her trade. She saw all the proper embalming items and noted they were in good condition, though she might need to buy a new trocar. There were shelves of polished steel full of everything she could possibly need. The room seemed to be fully stocked in chemicals and she felt relief seeing all the pink and orange fluid-filled bottles. She read through them and noticed her aunt was out of cavity fluid.

"Easy fix," she said to herself.

A computer and chair were the finishing touches, and thankfully her aunt had updated to an electronic system.

"I wonder if she put old data in here too?" She'd ask the

lawyer. She needed to go through the paperwork anyway to make sure she had all the passwords and such.

Both doors at the far end were large, wide enough to get a gurney or casket through. The doors were solid wood but easily opened.

Eyes widening with surprise as she opened the first door, she stepped onto a ramp. Following it up she came to another door. Opening this door led to the side of the house with the crematory and road.

"Clever," Thana said, much better than trying to get a body up and down the stairs.

This side of the house was much different than the others. The woods crept up almost touching the brick building with its metal doors. Tall trees of evergreen, thick and throwing shadows even in the mid-morning light. As a child, she'd never cared about wandering in the forest. Who wants the dangers of wild animals and getting lost when they had Forgotten Hills to play in?

There was no grass in the place, just gravel, gray and unforgiving. It smelled dusty and underused. This part of her new home was just not as vibrant and welcoming. She did notice a small path into the forest that looked intriguing. Maybe when Lola got there they'd go exploring, it might cheer her up.

Turning she went back down into the basement. The second door wasn't a mystery, it led to cold storage, a giant refrigerator for the dead. Thana walked in, shivering. She could see her breath and goosebumps were already rising on her skin.

"Hello! Thana?" Morana's voice came from the stairs.

Thana poked her head out. "What's up?" she called to her sister.

"Someone is here to see you, sending him down!"

Sighing Thana came out and shut the door. Who could be visiting them already?

"Who is it?" she asked, hoping whoever it was didn't offend easily.

"He says he's Lorelei's administrative assistant! That he's been taking care of the house!"

"Oh, ok!" The lawyer hadn't mentioned anything about an administrative assistant, but Thana was relieved to find there was one. Especially if he had been taking care of her aunt's property these past years.

He came down the stairs, a serious expression on his handsome face. He didn't smile at her and it was all she could do not to gape at him like an idiot.

"Draven?" she asked, amazement present in her voice. It couldn't be. He looked good. His hair was still dyed the weird silver color. He'd gotten much taller and was thin but muscular. He wore a red button-up shirt and black jeans Those pale green eyes of his didn't look happy to see her.

"Thana, you shouldn't have come back here," he said, voice soft and silky. It wasn't filled with the teasing lilt she remembered.

"What? Of course, I should have. It's mine now and it's perfect for what we need," she said, confused by his reception.

"I know. So, I'm here to help." He shoved his hands in his pockets.

"There's no way you were Lorelei 's assistant." Not after how she'd treated him twenty years ago. Plus, what thirty-five-year-old man spent his time catering to an aging mortician?

"I was...am...I handle the paperwork, ordering, the transport, and when she died, the upkeep. When I heard you were back and taking over Forgotten Hills, I thought you might need more than my handyman skills," he said, a cocky quirk to his mouth.

"Did you sit around the last five years hoping she'd left you Forgotten Hills?" That must be it, he was angry Lorelei hadn't given him the property.

"No, it stays in the Muerticillo family. I've been working in Portland, but my home is here as long as there is a job for me. I'd have stayed in Hill City if I could have gotten work," he said.

Thana took a moment to think, his statement went along with her guesses about his horrible home life. He probably did whatever was needed to pay the rent.

Did he remember kissing her? Had he really come to see her and spent the night fucking her? The thoughts whispered through her mind and she shook them away. He'd probably fucked a dozen girls since her if it hadn't been a drunken hallucination.

"And you were really her admin assistant?"

"Yes, your aunt was kind enough to send me to college."

She still didn't believe Lorelei had been so kind to a boy she'd seemed to despise once upon a time, but maybe things changed. Thana just wished they'd changed enough that they'd been invited back.

"Alright. I must admit I could use the help. Especially if you already know your way around," she said.

"Thank you, Forgotten Hills is like...home." His eyes darkened briefly.

"I have to say, it's nice to see you, Draven," she said, slowly, cautiously.

Delight flickered over his features and he smiled at her. "You grew up well, Thana. I know your aunt was proud of you."

"I kept your secret, you know." That seemed foolish to say now. "I never told anyone about you."

"I know."

Getting that out of the way she decided a businesslike approach was her best tactic.

"Can you start by making a few calls for me? I want to make sure this place is up to code and see about adding a garage and fixing up the crematory."

She wasn't prepared for the flash of anger on his features. She took a step back as his eyes went from coolly watching her to passionate fire in a second.

"You can't make changes to Forgotten Hills. Repairs, yes, but major changes like additions or taking down old structures are impossible."

"It's my home now and unless there's something legally binding, I don't see why not." She put her hands on her hips, staring him down.

"Just think about it. You might regret making changes later. I must go. I'll make those calls and get back to you." He left quickly. The only thing remaining the slight muskiness of his cologne.

Shaking off the oddness of Draven's visit, Thana went back to the morgue, eventually, she'd need to ask him about the night of her graduation. But what if he told her she was crazy? What if...

"Not now, Thana, put it behind you," she muttered her mantra. She needed to finish up her first inspection and meet Morana upstairs. They had to get Lola's room ready before she got there. She went back into the morgue.

She shivered again, this room was too cold, she was grateful for the cream-colored sweater she'd put on this morning. It shouldn't be this cold; a positive temperature morgue didn't feel like this. If she didn't know better, she'd swear this was a negative temperature room, which were used for forensic institutes.

Five body sized drawers filled the space and she was

happy to see she'd have enough room to take more than one client on at a time. Before moving she'd contacted the local hospital and nursing home to spread the news Forgotten Hills would be re-opening within a few months. They were all glad to hear it. She'd gotten the impression the locals didn't like sending their dead thirty miles down the road to be taken care of.

She opened the first drawer, empty and clean.

Thana really wanted to delve into her aunt's records to see just how busy she had been in the past. She knew that Forgotten Hills Cemetery wasn't used for burials and that residents of Hill City were buried in a new and much larger cemetery in between Hill City and its closest neighbor, Pineville.

She opened the second drawer and noticed that it squealed a little more than necessary, she either needed to replace the rollers or have them cleaned.

Thana had so many questions she wished Lorelei was alive to ask. Where did she order her urns and caskets from? Was it busy enough she needed help asides from Draven? Did she get business from anyone outside of Hill City? Who did the cleaning?

Opening the third drawer Thana's breath caught in her throat. Her hands dropped to her sides and mouth fell open. She didn't make a sound, just stared at the contents. She blinked rapidly, then closed her eyes. It had to be her imagination. She was too cold, too tired, too worried and too stressed to take what she saw at face value. She counted to ten and opened them again. It was still there.

Confusion, fear, and wonder filled her mind. She carefully shut the drawer and left the room going back to the stairs. As she climbed them, her mind began to scream at her.

How the hell did she tell Morana they already had a dead body to care for?

FOUR

THANA KNEW FROM THE START SHE WAS MEANT TO FOLLOW Lorelei's path. She wandered the cemetery more than her sisters. She memorized the epitaphs and the locations of every headstone. She kept a notebook full of names and dates. The only area she didn't go near was the one members of her family were buried in. Too morbid, even for her.

She stalked around the crematory, an odd combo of disgust, fear, and wonder swirling around in her belly. She would lean in, pressing her hands against the brick and imagine she could feel the heat from the oven inside. She would take deep breaths in through her nose to see if the gray smoke smelled oily and of meat, but it never did.

She found all the cemetery's hidden secrets. The hidey hole under the weeping angels, the blackberry bushes along the west side, how if you scraped your finger along one of the stones on the southeast wall you could ease it out and look into the forest beyond. She knew not to step too far left off the path past the gate after it rained because sometimes a small sinkhole formed. She knew if you stood in the right place at the right time it sounded like you were in a wind tunnel. Some of these things she shared with her sisters. Others she did not.

Lola got mad because Thana wouldn't play dolls and would rather write stories about the people laying beneath the thick green grass. Morana became easily annoyed that Thana wouldn't help make pancakes and instead ate breakfast in a corner where a wild blackberry bush grew. She would stain her fingers and leave kisses and fingerprints on some of her favorite headstones. Not to deface them, but so that the dead might know they were not forgotten.

Occasionally, while her sisters napped like sleepy kittens, she would make her way to the stairwell and listen to her aunt work. Sometimes her aunt would hum to herself, old tunes, new tunes, from time to time music Thana didn't recognize, old Spanish folk songs.

She would creep down a step at a time, her stomach a bundle of nerves. She wanted to see but always worried about bothering her aunt.

Then, abruptly, all would go silent and Thana would sit on the steps and wait. Lorelei's face would appear at the bottom of the stairs, kind and smiling.

Now and then she would come up and make tea and they would drink it together among the tombstones. Other times she'd say, "just checking on who was spying," laugh and go back to work. Mostly they talked. About it, about mom, about life.

They never had the same conversation twice and one was a favorite memory.

"What do you feel?" Lorelei asked.

"Nervous, butterflies in my stomach."

"No, not butterflies. With women like us, they are moths. Soft white moths fluttering. The flutters are ok, as long as you don't let them prevent you from doing something you want." Lorelei beckoned her to come closer and slowly Thana inched down, step by step. The basement was normally off limits, but in afternoons like these; where low gray clouds filled the skies and humid warmth filled the halls and the cemetery tasted of musk and rain, it wasn't so scary.

"What is it you want?" Lorelei asked. She stepped away from the stairs, disappearing into the basement so Thana couldn't see her anymore. A small partition blocked the preparation room from the stairs. Put there to protect tiny eyes from death.

"I want to come down and look," Thana finally declared, her young voice loud in the overwhelming quiet.

"Then come in."

Thana rounded the corner and there her aunt stood, a death goddess in her protective gear and gloves, perched next to equipment Thana didn't recognize. Thana tried to hide her disappointment that there wasn't a dead person.

She'd imagined gory messes of human remains, old wrinkled and cracked skin, ghastly scents and bloated figures stacked into corners.

This looked like a hospital.

"Disappointed?" Lorelei asked, amused.

The moths were back. Would Lorelei be horrified by her thoughts? Irritated?

"You want to see the dead, don't you, Querida?" Lorelei asked. Thana could only nod her head in excitement.

"I will show you, under one condition."

"Anything."

"You must never come down here without me and never enter the morgue without a grown up. Not until you are much older and have gone to college, yes?"

"Yes."

"So, it is actually a dead person?" Morana asked, jogging Thana from her memories They were sitting on the front porch drinking coffee. The roasted beans scent hinted with cinnamon wafted up from Thana's pale blue mug. The scent wrapped around trying to be comforting, it was almost successful.

Thana hadn't thought about how she had used berry juice to decorate headstones in a long time. While she never lost the fascination with death, she did lose the fantasy of it, how she used to believe death and Forgotten Hills had a real magic in it. She'd become a realist with a passion, outgrowing the child with a dream and a fairy tale.

"Yes, a real dead person," Thana said.

"Who?"

She'd told Morana last night about the body. Being Morana, she'd refused to go down and look. They'd decided not to deal with it until the next day, giving them plenty of time to finish making up the bedrooms and wrap their thoughts around why their aunt had a dead person in the freezer.

First thing this morning Thana went downstairs and opened the body bag up, to see who or what she was dealing with. It'd struck her around midnight the bag might not contain a body at all but money or jewelry.

"From what I can tell it's a young woman and she's frozen. Perfectly preserved. She's naked and has no identification."

"Super creepy, Thana." Morana took a sip of her own coffee, one hand against her leg tapping to an invisible beat, a nervous tick.

Prepared to do battle with dust, both girls wore jeans and t-shirts. Morana was barefoot, toes with blue paint also tapped on the porch, in a rocking pattern.

Thana feared getting dozens of splinters in her feet, the

porch really needed some work, so she had on a pair of orange slip-on loafers.

"Yes, but what do we do about it?" Thana asked. This cannot be happening again. One time her reputation could hold, but twice? Forgotten Hills was meant to be her haven, not a new nightmare.

"Call the local cops is my guess. They come out to take the body away and figure out why she's down there and how she died," Morana said it all very matter of fact.

"We could look through Lorelei's records here too," Thana said. Oh no. The cops would do a search and see her name associated with the Lottes.

"Ask that cute guy with the weirdo name, Draven, right? He left his number on the desk."

"Good idea, Draven might know."

"I feel uncomfortable being here with that dead girl downstairs." Morana took another drink of her coffee.

"That's ridiculous. Once this place is up and running there'll always be a dead person downstairs," Thana reminded her.

"This is different, this feels wrong," Morana muttered.

"Okay, you call the cops, I'll call Draven." Thana stood up, might as well get it over with. With any luck, this wouldn't affect her reopening. Hopefully, the girl wasn't murdered, and they all became suspects. Even more so, Thana worried her aunt had taken a body in right before her fall and forgotten to tell anyone about it. It would put an awful stain on Forgotten Hills if this was simply a job that never got finished. Thana could not deal with any more drama in her work or personal life.

Thana walked into the house, shoes leaving prints in the thick carpet. Leaning one hip against the desk she reached for the tiny white card, so crisp and clean that the green lettering stood out in stark contrast with Draven's first and last name followed by a phone number.

She fingered the card staring at the last name—Smith. That couldn't possibly be his real last name, could it? Not with a name like Draven before it.

Sliding her slim black cell phone from the pocket of her jeans she dialed the number, fumbling. She took a deep breath and lectured herself. She was much too old and too experienced to be acting like this over a guy, especially this guy.

He isn't just a guy, he's the guy, her traitorous mind said. *No, he's not.* She and her therapist had been over and over the fact she held every person she dated to Draven's standard. A boy she had been a little in love with at fifteen. A man she had, maybe, a one-night stand with. A silly fantasy providing a barrier to throw up so no one got too close to her. One she'd worked through and been done with for years. *Dani, oh Dani.* She bit her lip and shoved the thought into a closet and locked it.

Draven picked up on the first ring.

"What's wrong, Thana?" His voice was cold, but not distant cold, burning cold. Like when you touched ice for too long.

"How did you know it was me?" Thana asked.

"Caller ID, now what do you need?"

"Umm…I have an awkward question to ask you."

"No question you could ask me would be awkward." There was a hint of amusement in his voice.

"We…well, I…found a body in the basement."

"I'll be right over. Don't touch anything."

Thana blinked slowly at her phone, had he just hung up on her?

She went outside to see if Morana's call to the local police had gone any better. Her sister was sitting on the porch still, both their half-finished cups of coffee forgotten by her feet, cooling in the fall air.

Her sister was staring down at the phone in her hands, a dumbfounded expression on her face.

"What? Are the cops coming? Do they think we committed a crime?"

Morana looked up at her and confusion laced her features, "The Sheriff got on the phone with me. He told me to leave the body alone and if possible, forget we found it."

"What the actual fuck?" Thana sat down, heavily. "What does that even mean?"

"I think it means they know she's down there."

"But why would Lorelei leave a body down there? She's frozen solid and really well preserved."

"What did Draven say?" Morana asked, her face looked a little ashen.

"Nothing, he said he was coming by."

"This just gets weirder and weirder." Morana stood and stretched. "I'm going into the kitchen. Let me know if Draven has anything interesting to say. I want all of Lola's favorite foods made when she gets here."

"Of course." Thana nodded. Morana didn't want to deal with this issue, so she was retreating into the familiar—her baking.

Draven arrived shortly after Morana left. He looked just as he had the day before. He wasn't classically handsome, but there was something about him that drew her in. Something scary and sexy all at once.

She stood up to greet him, putting what she hoped, was a professional smile on her face.

He wore a brown and copper flannel shirt and jeans with large black boots, his hands were tucked in his pockets and he smiled at her, the same smile she remembered.

"Do you live close by?" She figured he had to have

walked unless he parked way down the road and walked in, but she doubted it.

"Yeah, I have a small house, that way." He motioned with his head, past the cemetery on the side where she'd first met him all those years ago.

They stood in silence, the awkwardness washing over them until Thana cleared her throat.

"The body," she said.

His eyes narrowed, "Yes, I figured you would find her, just not this soon."

"Stop the cryptic nonsense and just tell me what I need to know. Even the Sheriff gave Morana some ambiguous garbage." She crossed her arms over her chest.

"She's been there as long as I've known your aunt. Lorelei told me she wasn't to be disturbed in any way. That she had to remain under your family's care." His words were hesitant, and Thana got the impression he was choosing what he told her carefully.

"Ummm, and no one thinks that's strange? Shouldn't we just bury her? Do you know her name or anything about her?" Thana asked, feeling very uncomfortable with their conversation.

"No."

"What do you mean, no?" Was he joking? There were very strict laws about how remains had to be handled. Putting them in a freezer and forgetting about them were not on the list.

"Just what I said. Look, have you even glanced at the legal paperwork or her will?" He rubbed his temples, a tired sigh escaping his mouth.

Thana bristled, "The legal paperwork, yes. I haven't the heart to go into the will yet, it's mainly bequeathments and personal requests."

"I helped her write those, Thana. You may want to read

them. While she may not have legally bound you to keep the body or tied your hands regarding renovation, she did make requests regarding both subjects."

"Look, I get you are trying to help. However, I can't make this place run successfully again without updating. No way can Forgotten Hills compete with other mortuaries without some change." Thana took a step forward, hands out in a peaceful gesture, and was hurt when Draven took a step back.

"I love this place and I loved my aunt," she continued, "but Lorelei was quirky, and my mom says prone to flights of fancy. I can't in good conscience leave a body in the freezer indefinitely."

"Your mom says?" He snorted a laugh. "Maybe you should ask your mom why she left and about her birthmark. Lorelei was an amazing woman, a lot like you." His eyes darkened as he held her gaze.

Thana brushed her fingers over the red birthmark winding up from her wrist to her elbow, almost filigree in pattern.

"Mom didn't have a birthmark," she whispered. He'd told her this before. She never had the courage to ask and then she forgot all about it.

"All the women in your family do." He turned and began walking away. Just as she was about to call out to him, he stopped and gave her half his face, impressive jawline and strong nose.

"Wait," she called out to him, he couldn't know her history.

He stayed where he was.

"Did you read anything last year about a chain of funeral homes on the east coast closing?" A cold ache started in her belly; she didn't want to talk about this.

He turned back to her, frowning. "I think so, Lotte's Funeral Home, right?"

She nodded her head, squeezing her eyes shut. "Several

workers were charged with mishandling remains. The owners were found selling belongings and one of them was working on an expired license. They couldn't afford the fees, so they closed. It left a stain on most of the people that worked there." There, out fast, like ripping off a band-aid.

There was a pause, an audible lack of anything.

"I worked there, had for five years. I never knew anything shady was going on. I liked the Lotte's. I did my job and did it well. The investigation cleared me, but I still lost my job. I am still associated with that and I refuse to do it again. This body cannot stay here," she said.

Draven gave her an understanding look, but still he said, "she has to. I called a contractor I think you will like, and he will be here on Tuesday."

The day Lola comes, Thana thought as Draven disappeared behind the cemetery walls.

She spun on her heel and went into the house. She needed to read her aunt's last words and call her mother.

She stormed down the hall and into the kitchen which was a flurry of sights and smells. White flour, spicy cinnamon, melting butter and the heat from the oven.

"What's wrong?" Morana asked, flour on one cheek and the sparkles of sugar all over her shirt as she pushed dough into a ball.

"Draven said the same thing as the police, leave the body there, it's what Lorelei wanted."

"Too creepy, we have to get rid of it. It freaks me out, and what will Lola say?"

"He said Lorelei wrote very detailed requests in her will. And we just won't tell Lola."

"I didn't have the heart to read through the letters," Morana said, quietly. Her hands stopped moving as she engaged Thana.

"Draven also mentioned that mom has *it*."

This caused Morana to step away from the dough and wipe her hands on her apron, "That can't be possible. If she did, wouldn't she have helped us more?"

Thana could only shrug.

Morana stormed away from the kitchen and to the stairs.

"Wait, what are you doing?" Thana followed her sister.

"Calling Mom!"

"Wait, what?" Thana hurried after her, taking the stairs two at a time and was out of breath, panting, by the time she reached the living room.

"Morana, stop, you don't talk to Mom, remember?" She'd been begging her to for years, to reconcile, this was not how she pictured it.

"I will today!"

Morana was already in the small study that they'd called a library when they were young. The walls were covered in built-in shelves full of books and a small oak desk was crammed in a corner with the wobbly computer chair. Thana's laptop was plugged in, sitting open, the screen saver flashing stars and planets at them.

"If Lorelei talked to Draven, maybe it's true and if it's true we need to know." Morana sat at the computer and pulled up Skype. She dialed their parents. This was the easiest way to reach them because they were always abroad. Currently, they were exploring castles in Ireland.

Morana sat in the computer chair, Thana leaning down pushing against her shoulder, so they would both be in the video.

The Skype tone rang through the quiet room for about thirty seconds before their mother's face appeared on the other side. She was just an older version of Morana, minus *it*. Morana had cut her hair short just to be different from their mother.

"Morana! Oh, sweetheart...." Their mom trailed off,

probably from the storm cloud face Morana was giving her. She bit her lip and continued, "Is everything ok, is it Dolores?" Her rushed soft voice came through the speakers clearly. The worry evident in her wrinkled brow.

"Lola isn't due here for two more days, Mom. I told you that, didn't you get my email?" Thana asked.

"Yes, but if it's not Dolores, why are you calling?"

It was a valid question, aside from holidays, birthdays and big news they never called their parents, especially if they were traveling.

"We got some information today we need you to clarify," Morana said, a little contempt leaking into her words.

"Is that Morana?" The melodic tones of their father's voice drifted in. Mom turned away for a few minutes and they could hear muffled sounds of conversation, then their mom was back.

"You girls are already at Forgotten Hills?" she asked, ignoring Morana's previous statement.

"Yes, and we need to talk to you about something," Thana said.

Was it her imagination or did her mother tense up?

"Morana, sweetheart. I haven't spoken to you in two years, can we please not talk about that creepy old place?"

"And whose fault is that?" Morana asked. Thana placed a hand on her sister's shoulder, begging for calm.

"Mom, we just have a few questions, please?" Thana asked, as always, trying for peace.

"I don't know what you could have found in that moth-ridden dump that you need my help with." Resigned, mom settled into her chair and fixated on the screen.

"Did Lorelei and you have our birthmark?" Thana asked.

Their mother seemed to freeze and then her eyes focused above their faces, lips pursed.

"You know Lorelei did. It was a heart like blob on her shoulder, she liked to show it off when we were in school."

"And you?" Thana prompted.

"I don't know why it matters. Girls, you are stirring up the past and it's a past that need not be stirred," Mom said, anger creasing the corners of her eyes.

"Mom…" Thana said.

Their mother sighed and crossed her arms over her chest. "Like dogs with a bone," she muttered. "Fine. Yes, I do."

"Where? I've never seen it?" Morana asked. They were both surprised.

"Because I have taken great pains to ensure it is hidden. I hate it. All the people in my family have the mark. It is on my ass, if you must know."

"But the only thing on your ass is the rose tattoo…" Morana trailed off, eyes widening.

"I tried everything to get rid of it. Even a plastic surgeon told me he couldn't remove it and back then I couldn't hide it with make-up. I turned it into something tolerable. I covered it with red ink, and I get it touched up every few years because eventually, the mark starts to bleed through." She rubbed a hand over her eyes.

"I told you not to go there. My family is cursed, and the cemetery and mortuary should simply be burned to the ground."

"Why do you hate it so much?" Thana asked. She truly couldn't understand; Forgotten Hills was a beautiful piece of their history. Her mother's profession was all about history, how could she hate her own?

"If you stay there long enough, you will find out."

"Do you know about the body in the basement? The girl?" Thana asked.

"It's a mortuary, isn't it supposed to have dead people in it?" she countered, an obvious deflection.

"Oh, please, Mom, just answer the question," Morana snapped.

"Yes, I know about her and I won't say another word on the matter. In fact, unless you'd like to speak to Dad, this conversation is now over. We'll be home for Christmas if you would like to spend it with us. Please have Dolores call me when she gets there." She paused and her whole demeanor softened for a second. "It was lovely seeing you, Morana, I miss you. I love you girls, be safe."

"Love you too, Mama," they said at the same time and the screen went black.

FIVE

Four Years Ago

MORANA AND TRIXIE WERE MARRIED ON A MUTED LATE September afternoon. The air smelled clean, fresh and woodsy. They chose a lovely outdoor venue in Happy Valley, Oregon. Everything was green, tinged in gold, bronze, and orange as fall made her appearance. The sun was just starting to set so that the splash of color would be behind the brides as they said their vows.

White chairs filled a brown loam area creating the aisles. White gossamer hung from anything that would hold still. Twinkling lights were strung through the trees and oil lamps burned sweetly to stave off any encroaching darkness or bugs.

The reception would be held in a historic white trimmed building on the property, filled with long tables and soft lighting. The rich aromas of vegetarian delights and traditional Spanish desserts tickled the nose as you walked in. Their cake was huge and white covered in sugar spun flowers and sections that were painted like stained glass. Inside was a ginger spice cake with a grand Marnier cream.

The table centerpieces were overflowing with maple leaves, thistles, hydrangeas, orange roses, and white mini orchids. There were tiny printed menus at each place setting and champagne flutes with the wedding date etched in gold. A table on one side held a mountain of presents while one across the room held chocolate boxes for each guest to take home.

Lola and Thana walked with Morana as she took her place at the front, standing under a simple and elegant wedding arch. She was dashing with her makeup on, hair slicked to one side, held in place by a barrette of thistles and wearing a black dress with a white belt. As they waited for the ceremony to start, they watched as people began filling the chairs. Murmurs of conversation washed over them.

Morana smiled brightly as she watched the seats fill, but after each minute her smile dimmed until a frown was pursed on her bronze slicked lips.

"They aren't here," Morana whispered to her sisters, facing away from her guests, lips barely moving.

Thana scanned the crowd; the seats up front they saved for their parents were empty.

"We didn't know if they were coming, you knew that," Lola said, wrapping an arm around their younger sister.

"I thought, I hoped..." Morana couldn't finish the words. She was fighting back tears.

"They never returned their RSVP. I called them, and Mom wouldn't give me a straight answer. I hoped they'd put their feelings aside, especially since they sent a gift," Thana said. She moved to stand in front of Morana. She crossed her eyes and stuck out her tongue.

Morana gave a small bark of laughter, straightening her shoulders, she blinked rapidly.

"They hate that I'm marrying a woman this much?"

"It doesn't fit in with what they wanted for us. They will come around, I promise," Lola said.

"And it doesn't matter, we're here and we are what's most important." Thana did a tiny dance and hoped no one was watching. It had the intended effect and Morana smiled.

"I am never speaking to them again if they don't show up," Morana promised.

"If that's how you feel," Lola whispered, "then we shall respect that."

Music began to play, beautiful and soft, but you could tell it was Hold Me, Thrill Me, Kiss Me by Mel Carter.

"It's starting!" Thana said, excitement in her voice.

The three of them turned to watch as Trixie came down the aisle, each of her parents holding an arm.

———

Tuesday came too soon. Morana and Thana busted their asses to get everything ready for their sister's arrival. They redecorated her room with all new, clean, fresh smelling and beautiful things using Lola's favorite color, pale yellow and filling vases full of sunflowers.

They stocked the fridge, pantry, and freezer with her favorite foods and everything they would need to have meals together like a family.

There were still a few things to do, but the living quarters and family rooms were as close to perfect as they could be in a little over a week.

They both tried to ignore the strange dead girl in the basement. Thana reached back out to the police and tried to pester Draven again, but both were, excuse the pun, dead ends.

Instead, Thana threw herself into Lorelei's private papers. The legal documents were straight forward. She and her sisters owned the mortuary, cemetery and a few acres of property around them. A large sum of money had also been left to divide among the three of them. Almost a million dollars.

Legally the only thing she couldn't do was move the bodies from the cemetery or sell it. Her aunt's lawyer was shark-like.

The intensity of Lorelei's will stunned her. While not legally binding, it did make Thana feel a bit like an ungrateful ass to go against her requests.

Lorelei requested no major renovations or improvements be made aside from fixing items that were broken, rotted, unsafe or no longer up to code. She requested that the main structures including the cemetery and crematorium not be altered in any way. After that, the requests became crazier.

"Did she lose her mind at the end?" Morana asked as they read a paragraph demanding they stay away from the woods to the east and not cover their birth marks.

Another section warned them about strangers in town and how they had a duty to keep the people of Hill City safe.

There was a brief passage discussing the girl in the basement a simple sentence: *Do not move the girl in the basement; simply let her be and forget she exists.*

Anxiety beat in Thana's chest like a wild thing every time she thought about the dead girl. If anyone found out they were sure to link it to her past and her hopes of starting fresh would dissolve. Her reputation couldn't handle another scandal, even if she hadn't done anything wrong.

Thana was on the hunt for personal records, hopefully, there was more of an explanation in a file somewhere or hidden away in some of her aunt's things.

This meant spending time downstairs on the computer, digging through her aunt's files. The cold basement and clean, clinical environment's chemical smell was like an old friend.

She never felt more comfortable with herself than when she was in a preparation room. She could forget about the strange girl in the freezer a few feet away.

"The contractor is here, Thana!" Morana called from the kitchen.

Excitement bubbled in her stomach, finally, she could get started on the business section of this adventure. Grabbing her list from next to the computer she hurried up the stairs. She was wearing a black pant suit with a violet collared shirt, wanting to appear professional, rather than casual.

Coming out into the front room she saw Draven sitting at the receptionist desk, looking amazing in a white suit jacket, black slacks, and a black shirt.

"What are you doing here?" she asked, coming to a sudden halt.

"We are conducting business today? You need a full staff. Unless you don't want the help, that is." The smile he gave her was gentle.

She took a moment to consider. From the payroll and tax files she'd browsed this morning she knew Draven had worked for Lorelei. She'd been giving him a paycheck for ten years, including a few holiday bonuses. The computer in the receptionist area was prestigiously organized and linked to the one downstairs, which she assumed was all Draven's work. She'd never seen such a well put together office before. Everything she could ever want was electronically categorized and easily searchable.

Her aunt's personal files were much more scattered.

"Yes, of course, I'd love to keep you on, Draven. I was just surprised to see you, is all."

"I told Lorelei we needed an intercom system, but she liked not being bothered while she worked," he said.

"I will add that to the list. I don't get great reception

downstairs, so an intercom and possibly business Skype would be good," she agreed.

"Don't worry, I'll take care of it," Draven said.

"Morana said the contractor was here?" If he was, maybe he was an invisible contractor? Because he wasn't in the waiting room.

"He wouldn't come inside, he's out on the porch." Draven waved toward the door.

"Why?"

"He's not from Forgotten Hills, he's from Pineville and apparently it's a popular rumor that Forgotten Hills is haunted. Though he doesn't know any actual stories."

Thana laughed, "Haunted? I never saw one scary thing here. I like to think this place is magical, but not haunted. Why did he take this job then?"

"I know the family. He's good at what he does, and they need the money. I'm sure he'll get over it eventually. If it becomes a problem, let me know." Draven seemed distracted by something on the computer and his body language hinted that he wanted to be left alone to work.

Thana crossed the room and went out the door, onto the sun lit porch. A man stood in front near the house, pacing. He was short and wearing a fedora, with very tanned skin and an aquiline nose. He had on a tan suit the exact shade of his hat.

He grinned at her when she came out and bowed, sweeping the hat off to show a gleaming bald head.

"Ms. Muerticillo?" The rest of his sentence was lost on her as a rush of Spanish came from his mouth.

Trying not to be annoyed she said, "I am so sorry. I don't speak Spanish."

Standing, he clutched his hat with one hand and reached out with the other. "I am sorry, with your last name, I assumed...I am pleased to meet you."

She met him and shook his hand with firm resolve and returned his smile.

"I'm Dorian Garcia," he said, releasing her fingers.

Up close she could see a certain handsomeness in his features and guessed his age to be around fifty.

"Thank you for coming, Mr. Garcia, and please, it's simply Thana."

"And I am simply Dorian. Mr. Smith said you have some renovations you'd like to do with Forgotten Hills, and I am more than happy to assist you." He put his hat back on.

"Yes, though if you won't even come inside, I don't see how I can hire you," Thana said, with a frown.

"I know. It is silly. I grew up hearing odd tales about this place and the cemetery. I assure you it will not affect my work." He looked sheepish.

"It's not a lot. I want the house inspected and everything updated and brought up to code. I want broken items fixed, run down items replaced and dull items brightened. You will need to look at the crematory. I want to keep the equipment but completely rebuild the structure. I also don't want to be broke when we're done." She gave a small laugh.

She led him to the brick crematory, it's rough construct and muted colors in sharp contrast with the forest encroaching around it.

Dorian walked around the building and a low whistle slipped out of his thin lips. "I can see why you'd want to rebuild. This place probably would crumble down around whatever is inside."

Thana went to the black metal door and used a large brass key to unlock it and push it open. "I'd like keyless entry and to make this as modern as possible, a viewing room would also be a good addition," she said as she showed him around.

The large silver crematory oven was a brand-new addition to the room. She walked over to it and placed a hand on it. It was cool to the touch, and she hoped she could soon remedy that with clients. A macabre thought, but not cruel. Cream and brown wood cabinets and cupboards lined one wall. The tan colored remains processor sat among cleaning supplies and instruments she would need to catalog, clean and organize.

According to her records, Lorelei had purchased all new equipment the year before her fall as if trying to keep the place relevant. Thana was grateful for her aunt's foresight.

Hearing a car coming up the lane, something inside Thana tightened.

"Can you manage from here?" she asked, anxiety skittering through her bones.

"I'll make a few notes and head out. I will need to come back with a small team to assess the main house and property. I will have some preliminary blueprints and quotes for you by Monday," Dorian said, but he was distracted. He had out a pencil, paper and a measuring tape.

"Sounds good, just close the door when you're done. I will lock up later. Not much to steal in here anyway." Thana tried for a chuckle, but by the look on Dorian's face, she failed.

Quickly, she made her way back to the house, reaching it just as the old white Toyota Camry pulled into a parking space in-between Dorian's large blue pickup truck and her red Rav4.

Dust from the road swirled around the car, bringing an earthy smell and a brown tinge to the air.

Morana was already on the front porch. "She needs a new car."

Thana nodded in silent agreement and rushed over to the driver's seat to open the door.

Thana reached in to help the driver out and had her hands smacked away.

"If I can't get out of the car, then I need to go back to the hospital," a soft, pleasant voice said from behind dark sunglasses, bandages and bruises turning from deep purple to sickly green.

Thana glanced over the car's roof to Morana. They were thinking the same thing, she looked better than the last time they'd seen her, but not by much. Morana leaned down and tapped the passenger seat window.

"Unlock the doors and I'll start unloading your stuff."

Lola hit the unlock button with her right hand, her left was no longer in the sling, but Thana could tell it hurt by the way she was holding it.

The back seat was packed with garbage bags and boxes full of Lola's things. Everything that she could get was crammed in her tiny car and it wasn't much.

Lola had her straw-colored hair in a messy side braid and was wearing gray sweatpants and a blue t-shirt. The clothes were not something her sister would normally wear. In fact, Thana couldn't remember a time she'd ever seen Lola in anything so boring and mundane. They didn't look like they fit either.

"Lola, do you not have any clothes of your own?" Thana asked, softly, as Lola got out, wincing the entire time. She held herself at a funny angle and Thana knew it was because her ribs were still healing, as were other things.

"Some, nothing I wanted to drive in. I only had an hour or so and other things were more important," she answered.

"Bastard," Morana hissed, arms full of charcoal colored plastic.

Lola closed the doors and took off her sunglasses. Her pale blue eyes were wide in her face and looked shell shocked, even though her smile had a quirky up-turn. She was trying to make them think everything was all right, like always.

"Forgotten Hills looks wonderful, like a magical

getaway." She gave a long sigh and Thana put her arm around her shoulder.

"It needs some work, but once you walk into the cemetery it's as amazing as when we were kids."

"Good, but first, my room? I feel like I could sleep for a week."

Thana took Lola inside, passing the horse paintings and making their way to the grim little hallway that would take them into a more pleasant environment.

Draven looked up from his desk and Thana was pleased with how quickly he masked his shock.

"Draven, this is my sister, Dolores. Draven is my administrative assistant."

Lola stiffened against Thana and gave a slight head tilt in his direction. "Nice to meet you."

"It's a pleasure. Thana told me you would be moving in with her. I hope you enjoy Forgotten Hills," he said, catching Thana's gaze, his own ripe with questions.

"Come on," Morana said, ignoring Draven. She pushed the door to the hallway open and led the way into the kitchen.

Thana made a mental note to repaint, hang some photos and install some lights. It was creepy to go from the warm, pleasing waiting room, meant to console the bereaved, into a dark little hallway and out again into a friendly kitchen.

"You didn't tell me about him," Lola accused.

"I didn't know until we got here. He's been working with Lorelei for years. He knows how everything runs," Thana explained.

"I could do office work for you," Lola said.

"Nope, you are here to rest and relax and put things back together." Morana paused in the kitchen, watching Lola's expression.

"If he bothers you, I'll fire him, but right now he's being helpful." Thana kept the other thoughts from forming words.

Things like, *and I've known him forever. There's something about him that I can't get out of my mind. I need to find out what he knows about the girl in the basement. I had sex with him while you were down the hall once.... I think.*

"No, no. I'm just being silly," Lola said.

"You are not silly. Now, are you hungry? We have everything! Macaroons, corned beef, rye bread, pickled asparagus, churros, and frozen mozzarella sticks! All your favorites. I even baked several macaroon flavors; grape, root beer float, and chocolate. Everything you love," Morana said.

"You overdid it and I appreciate it, but right now I would like to go lie down," Lola said, bags under her eyes. She yawned and gave a slight giggle as it contagiously made its way through Morana and Thana.

"Mom wants you to Skype her," Thana mentioned as she led the way upstairs and toward the room facing the driveway.

"Later," Lola said. Then she stopped in the doorway and turned to her sisters, tears welling up in her eyes.

"What?" Morana dashed into the room, putting down the trash bag and looking around to see what had offended her.

"It's perfect, I can't believe you guys did all this for me," Lola sobbed, wrapping slim arms around Thana.

Morana made a noise somewhere between a gasp and a cry and hugged them both. They tried to be delicate and not hurt Lola, but it had been a while since they'd all been together like this. The hospital room didn't count.

Thana felt a deep longing in her stomach as a burning behind her eyes took all her focus not to give in to. She could smell the inner mingling scent of her sisters, together they smelled like summer in Forgotten Hill—Quesitos pastries and coconut lemonade with a hint of antiseptic.

"It's all right, Lola, you're home. Lie down and Morana and I will bring in the rest of your things." Thana placed a kiss on the top of her head.

"Here, let me help you." Morana took their sister's arm, gingerly and led her to the bed with the brand-new buttercup yellow bedding.

Thana left them there, heading back down to the car. She knew Lola would feel better if she could be around some more of her things. She hoped she'd managed to get her sewing and art supplies from the house.

"Is she okay?" Draven asked, eyes meeting hers and she came into the room.

"She will be." Thana sighed and sank into one plushy green chair along the wall.

Draven waited patiently, eyes calm and sympathetic. He didn't pry, he just sat in silence with her for a few minutes.

She wanted to talk to him, she hadn't had a friend like Draven ever again. It's hard to trust people and make lifelong acquaintances when you jump from one school to the next. It's even harder when school is online in a foreign country because your parents can't find somewhere to store you while they vacation.

She wanted to ask him about that night, had she dreamed him? Had he really come to her and fucked her senseless?

She felt fifteen again, meeting him in their special space, worried that he snuck away from an abusive home life and aching to share her day with him. It was stupid, but in her gut, she knew no matter how cool and collected he acted toward her, Draven felt the same way.

She lifted her head and spoke. "A month ago her husband of eight years pushed her down a flight of stairs."

A growl came from Draven's mouth. It sounded inhuman, and his eyes flashed with anger. "I see."

Thana frowned but continued, "She was four months pregnant." She could only whisper the words and sorrow filled every space in her body. She remembered how excited Lola was to tell them they were going to be aunties. How she did yoga, ate healthy and never missed an appointment. She started picking out names and buying a few select pieces of clothing and décor.

"We didn't know...we should have known... We found out he'd been abusive for years, little things to start; gripping her arm until it bruised, telling her she was fat, not wanting her to leave the house. Insulting her Hispanic heritage. She admitted it escalated to marital rape and he broke her wrist a year ago." Thana had to pause, to get over her guilt and remember that now they were going to make sure nothing ever happened to their sister again.

"He decided the baby wasn't his, accused her of cheating. Thankfully, their maid was home and saw it all. She called 911 and he was arrested. She was just released from the hospital a few days ago. He'd already made bail and was back at home working, awaiting a trial date. She showed up while he wasn't home and had a few hours to pack up and leave," Thana finished.

"Why was she worried? With a restraining order, she could have simply had him arrested again."

"I wish it worked like that. My sister found out she wasn't on any of the household documents and he'd gotten back to the house before her. Fighting him for the right to reside in her home just wasn't going to happen. The maid called her when he left. She packed what she could and took off."

"So, did she steal the Toyota outside?" Draven asked, his tone implying he was trying to lighten the mood.

Thana did chuckle before speaking, but it was a dark sardonic sound, deep in her throat.

"No, she bought it. You never see Lola coming. She's an excellent seamstress and an even better painter. He didn't know, didn't know she'd been selling pieces over the past few years. She'd been planning to leave him. Had a bank account he didn't know about with a few thousand dollars in it. She filed for divorce from her hospital bed and we're using inheritance money to pay her lawyer. Not everyone is as lucky."

"I'm glad she made it here without incident," Draven said. "Don't worry about her husband; karma will catch up with him."

"I wish it could be the karma of me embalming him alive." It was an evil sentence, and it tasted good in her mouth; the words were like deep fried chocolate bars on her tongue.

Draven gave her a smile that was wanton and predatory all at once, but it was gone in a flash, so quickly she thought she only imagined it. She hungered for her brother-in-law's death and for a second that hunger was mirrored on Draven's face.

SIX

Summers in Forgotten Hills consisted of so much more than long lunches in the cemetery and intricate family dinners in the cozy kitchen.

Thana imagined her parents thought they were spending their days sunning themselves on the porch or with noses buried in books. Which they were.

A small girl could easily squish among the canned goods in the pantry and hide away in the dark.

A child could shimmy out a window and climb onto the roof hidden from view and listen to a variety of boy bands on her Walkman.

On very hot days they would lie on the ground in the cool pantry licking honey from their fingers as they snuck dulce de coco (coconut fudge), grateful for a cold cement floor beneath them.

However, they were also very busy with a variety of lessons from Lorelei.

Even as a baby, Morana loved to sink chubby fingers into the dough and would gleefully laugh as sugar and flour went everywhere.

As she got older it became easier to teach her the alphabet and her numbers if you could do it while cooking.

Lorelei's cooking style was much different than their mother's. Her food was a mix of their history; Spain, Mexico, and Puerto Rico, as well as many American dishes. Their mother only made "normal" food; pot roast, spaghetti, hamburgers, chicken noodle soup, etc.

Eating at Forgotten Hills was like being immersed in their genealogy.

Lorelei used recipes from dead ancestors; a Spanish great grandmother, another from a Mexican great uncle and some from their maternal Puerto Rican grandmother, to name a few.

Lola and Thana would sit patiently at the kitchen table while Lorelei cooked, a small step ladder by her side for Morana to climb upon.

They ate a few burnt cookies and under done pies before Morana really got a handle on things.

Lorelei was patient and calm, she went over steps again and again. She wrote down every recipe in a deep blue notebook, her loopy handwriting a never-ending flow of ink. Many of her recipes graced the menu at Morana's bakery: Forgotten Sweets.

Thana and Lola learned a little too, but neither had the passion for it that Morana did. When she went off to culinary school, it was simply what she was always meant to do. Their parents had wanted her to get a Doctorate in Business. Their father thought a bakery was a waste of her skills. Morana is a supreme businesswoman. She had been at eight with her first lemonade stand and she was now twenty-eight with a thriving business in downtown Portland.

Thana watched her sister bustle around the kitchen cleaning, after she'd finished whipping up the most delicious biscuits and gravy.

"Is Lola coming down for breakfast?" Thana asked, but she knew the answer.

"No, I'm going to take her a tray."

"I'm going to go downstairs and examine that body today, see if she has any clues on her. Check more files. If we're going to bury her, I'd at least like a name," Thana said.

"You sure that's a good idea?"

"You got a better one?"

Morana braced her hands against the counter and closed her eyes. She wasn't wearing her makeup and *it* stood bright against her cheek. "No, but so far two people are telling us to leave her alone."

"Without telling us why. I'm not going to be unethical unless it's for a good reason. A body should not stay frozen unless it's absolutely necessary," Thana said. She believed this with her whole heart. The dead had their place just like everyone else. After she was done with them, they belonged either in the fire or in the ground, sometimes in the water or a tomb. No matter how you chose to do it they belonged at rest. Sitting frozen in time in a sterile freezer was not appropriate. This woman was a living human being once, with thoughts, feelings, hopes, and dreams. She was a daughter, maybe a mother or a wife. It was disrespectful to ignore her and leave her cold and alone in a black bag.

"You didn't do anything wrong, Thana," Morana said quietly, staring at her sister, understanding her all too well.

"I know that. I also know I should have figured it out. I should have known something was up. I won't make the same mistakes again."

"How could you have known?"

"I loved Dani. I ignored the warning signs because I loved her. I should have seen it," Thana said, biting her lip. She didn't want to talk about it.

Morana stared at her for a few long seconds.

"Let's just not talk about it in front of Lola," Morana said and she went back to scrubbing the counter, the scent of bleach filled the air making everything smell clean.

Thana went downstairs; the lights were on and she stood in the middle of the prep room and just listened. It was quiet, the brief hum from the freezer and computer's mechanical whir the only sounds. It was nice, comforting. Everything about this room was perfect from the smell to the aesthetics.

Eyes focusing on the freezer's large metal door, she grabbed a sweater from the back of her computer chair and slapped on latex gloves and a mask. She opened the door and a burst of cold air hit her directly as well as the scent that all morgues seemed to carry—a metallic twisting of cleaning products and death.

Leaving the door open, she grabbed a gurney and moved it down the path between the crypts and the wall, parking it next to the one she wanted.

She opened the third drawer and pulled it out, a small grunt escaping her as her arms strained. It was a satisfying feeling, to use her strength and muscles. There was the dead girl, encased in a body bag and full of mystery.

With a few physical maneuvers and the work of some very useful equipment, Thana moved her to the gurney. She was out of breath and had some perspiration on her face, but it wasn't as difficult to do by herself as she imagined. Lorelei really had set this place up wonderfully. Thana knew after a dozen bodies or so she'd be so used to the physical labor, it would become a familiar if not relaxing routine.

Thana wheeled her into the main room, the clanking wheels echoed against the cement walls. Gripping the zipper, she unzipped the bag to reveal the girl within.

She was naked, dark skin blemish free and smooth. Not a freckle or a birthmark dotted her skin. There was a white scar on one knee and her chin. In Thana's opinion, probably childhood injuries.

She was somewhere between twenty and thirty with a narrow face that wasn't beautiful per se but not one easily forgotten either. Her cheek bones were high and nose crooked. She had a wide forehead and lush lips a natural blush color, with some blueish discoloration.

Thana was amazed at how well preserved she was, no bruising on her back or bottom to show blood pooling, she must be conserved somehow. Perhaps her aunt had done the embalming herself. Thana looked for a wound in her neck, large cut sewn with thick black thread, but could find none, another piece to the puzzle.

It was possible if she were frozen moments after death, she could look this perfect, almost alive. If Thana were prone to flights of fancy, she could imagine the girl might take a breath and sit up.

Her eyelashes sat dark against her cheeks and matched the deep brown of her hair, which was in a thick braid curling around one side of her neck and laying over her shoulder against her arm.

As Thana circled her, she noticed a speck of color on her right hip that wasn't visible from the other side. It was a tattoo of some sort that went from hip bone to her bottom. Curious she leaned down and pushed the girl's frozen skin to bring the entire picture into view.

It was a pale green circle with a line down the center that then had one side divided in half, with another horizontal line, making one large section and two little ones.

"What are you doing?"

Thana spun around, surprised. Draven was standing behind her with a look of anger and horror on his face. His words were filled with contempt.

"I'm looking at her. If there is a reason my aunt kept her down here, then I want to know what it is."

"You have no right. She is to be cared for and kept safe. Not for you to pull out, prod and poke, denying her death dignity."

He sounded like she had personally insulted him. He crossed the floor and put himself between Thana and the dead woman.

"Dignity? There's none of that lying frozen in a sterile crypt. She deserves to be buried. The only respect for the dead we have is our ability to take care they are properly laid to rest," Thana argued.

Draven faced the body and his eyes fell closed. He raised a pale hand and placed it on her cheek, mumbling something Thana couldn't hear.

"What?" Thana asked, bothered and intrigued with how tenderly he caressed the girl's face.

"She's already starting to thaw, so you must put her back. I can't even imagine the consequences of these actions." He lifted his strange green eyes to hers and she saw pleading in them. "Please."

It was that pleading and his demeanor of protectiveness for the dead that convinced her to do as he asked, but she still would get answers.

"All right, I'll put her back, but I don't understand what's going on. I don't like not knowing something that seems important." She went to the gurney and zipped the girl back up. The zipper made a harsh sound in the quiet room and Thana froze. It was impossible, but had the dead girl's eyes just moved?

The breath seemed to leave her body and time slowed down as she scrutinized the girl again. Cool air flowed over Thana as if she'd left the morgue open. The chill seeped inside her white and icy.

Then time seemed to speed back up. Draven stood across the way watching her solemnly. Thana shook off her macabre thoughts and finished closing the bag. She hated that her fingers were shaking and jammed them in the pockets of her dark green jumper. Looking toward the morgue she saw the doors were closed. Had she imagined it?

"Help me?" she asked, desperate to be done. She wanted to go upstairs to warmth and her sisters.

It was easier to get her back in with two people, but the quiet between them unnerved Thana.

"I can't tell you what's going on, but I know someone who can," Draven said as they left the morgue, shutting the cold in where it belonged.

"Who?"

"Here." Draven handed her an envelope. It was crisp and white. Her name was scrawled across it in her aunt's large and looping hand.

"She gave me this to give you if you started asking questions."

Thana stopped moving, simply clutching the letter in one hand. They stared at each other for a moment and then Draven lifted a hand. Barely touching her he tucked a strand of her midnight hair behind one of her ears. For a brief second, she felt the warmth of his skin and his touch caused moths to erupt in her stomach, fluttering around with fury.

She blushed, remembering how she'd hastily thrown her hair in a bun this morning. Why couldn't this have happened a few days before, when she was immaculately put together?

"I have to go," Draven said, and go he did.

Thana wasted no time. She ripped open the envelope and began to read.

Querida,
As clichéd as it is: If you are reading this, I am dead. I

am gone without telling you many things you need to know, and poor Draven is forbidden from telling you. I hope you never get this far, that you respect the wishes in my will and leave well enough alone.

I know this to be the wishful thinking of an old woman. I did not leave it alone and neither did your mother or your grandmother. So, I instructed Draven to give you this in case you dug your heels in.

Her name is Dabria Muerticillo and she is twenty-five years old. As you know, Hill City was established in the early 1800s by people from Spain and Puerto Rico. They came to Oregon and pumped money as well as blood and sweat into founding the town, making it thrive.

In 1845 a plague swept through Hill City and it started killing the very young and old. By then our family was well known as the caretakers of Forgotten Hills Cemetery and the funeral and mortuary business was just starting up.

By 1845, Dabria was married with three children. Her husband died shortly after the birth of their fourth child, a son who was taken by the plague. In her extreme grief, she believed sacrificing herself would cause the curse on the town to end.

Which it did. After her death, there were no other deaths from the plague or illness at all. Those who had been sick got better and the people believed Dabria gave them this gift. Unfortunately, because they were Catholic, suicide meant Dabria could not be buried at Forgotten Hills. Instead, the women of her family cleaned her, and they spent their days packing her in ice and snow until a proper freezer could be built to store her.

For a while people came to see her, to kiss her frozen lips and pray. It became a legend and strangers would show up at their doorway. Finally, they hid her away, telling everyone they had finally buried her in the woods.

Our family keeps her to this day because she is still a legend. If you stay at Forgotten Hills long enough someone will eventually come calling looking for, as they call her, Chica Que Cura La Muerte, or The Girl Who Cures Death. Don't believe me? Do an internet search, her real name isn't usually listed but the story is there, though over time it has been warped. Most people think they are looking for a child, not a grown woman. People, normally terminally ill and a little crazy, latch onto this story and try to find her. We could bury her in secret, but the fear is that someday someone would find her and desecrate her.

Keep Dabria safe and above all else, do not disturb her slumber.

Love,
  Aunt Lorelei

SEVEN

"Why don't we have dad's last name?" Morana asked one summer. She was six and perched on the counter, jam on her fingers as Lorelei made dough. Their aunt's large, strong hands pushed and pulled, kneaded and rolled the yeasty white mess until it began to resemble something akin to food.

The scent of flour and raw dough filled the room. It was middle morning and sunlight streamed in, causing dust particles to dance and sway with the breeze from the small box fan in the corner.

Thana could smell the hot metal from the oven pre-heating. She felt pulses of heat wash over her even as the fan blew lukewarm air in her direction. She sat cross-legged in the middle of the table, book in her lap. Lola lay sprawled beneath, fingers covered in charcoal, the sound of her scratching a soothing background noise.

"Tradition, I told you that," Thana said, annoyance in her voice. This got her a sharp look from their aunt. Thana ducked her head sheepishly. Lorelei often told her to watch her tone around her sisters. Over the years Thana's teenage hormones began controlling her voice, not just her body.

Morana stuck her tongue out at her when their aunt looked away.

"Our family is a giant Hodgepodge of different Hispanic cultures and mom broke the rules when she married a white guy," Thana said.

"Thana…" Lorelei warned.

"She's right though," Lola said, voice drifting from under the table, muffled, "it's just tradition. That's why Mom didn't take Dad's name."

"Well, that is partially correct," Lorelei said. Thana turned to watch her, how her aunt was holding her body, the inflection in her words were all the signs that Lorelei was about to tell them something they didn't know.

They waited for her to continue, three young eager faces watching her.

"Your mother is a professional, an academic. She did not want your father's last name attached to hers. She wants the credit for her work and respect that she may not get if she was simply Mrs. Burke. Especially with your father's reputation and fame in his field," Lorelei said. Thana knew Morana wouldn't really understand and that Lola would ask her to explain the points she missed later.

"That still doesn't explain why we aren't Burkes," Thana said.

"You're still Burkes, you are Muerticillo's and Burkes—a beautiful combination. Your parents chose to give you our family name so that you could find your own way and not rest in your father's family shadow," Lorelei explained. But Thana watched their aunt. She wasn't telling them something.

"You've left something out," she said. Lorelei's eyes met hers with surprise. She took a deep breath and laughed.

"You never miss anything, do you, Querida?"

Thana said nothing, she simply waited.

Morana licked deep purple jam from one finger and the

scritch-scratch under the table paused, along with what felt like time.

"Forgotten Hills is a family inheritance. It can only be inherited by someone carrying the Muerticillo name."

Time sped back up and all three girls laughed at the solemn look on their aunt's face.

"Well if that's all, no worries!" Lola exclaimed, "Thana will never change her last name. So she can have Forgotten Hills!"

Lorelei got a pan and began putting the bread dough into it, she flicked flour-dusted fingers at Morana. "Did that answer your question, Pequeña?"

"Yes, now when will this bread be toast?"

———

The dust from the construction was thick. Thana stood watching as the workers pulled down the old building with a sense of anxiety and hopefulness. In the last week, the house had sung with the noises of work. All day there were mumbled voices in a variety of tones and accents, clanging, banging and sawing from 7 a.m. to 5 p.m.

Smells of drywall, dust, paint, and sweat permeated the rooms and lingered on the air outside. After the full house inspection, the quote had been less than she'd thought and the work not as extensive. Dorian told her he'd have everything done in about two months.

"It's so loud, why are you out here?" Lola asked, coming from behind her. She looked better, some bruises were gone, and she was getting around easier.

"I just wanted to watch it come down. I can't wait to see the new building and get to work again," Thana said. She put an arm around Lola, and they walked toward the main house. Thana looked longingly through the gates at the cemetery.

They'd been so busy she'd only been once. It was just as she remembered, if not a bit overgrown. She'd hired gardeners to come put it back the way it used to be.

Draven sat at his desk as they walked by. He glanced up and smiled. "The intercom's being installed this afternoon and several people have called about an official opening date."

"Excellent. I am hoping in just over a month. But I'd hate to put out an official date just yet. Tell people before the holidays for sure."

"Your aunt used to do a monthly walk through the cemetery on the lookout for vandalism or repairs. I was going to do it this evening before I leave. Would you care to join me?" he asked.

Thana took a moment to consider. She felt Lola stiffen under her arm and knew that Draven made her uncomfortable.

He was funny and intense. She didn't care for the secrets he harbored, but their working relationship was turning into a grown-up version of their youthful friendship. In secret, she wouldn't mind if that included sex, but that was probably pushing it. Whether it had been an alcohol-fueled dream or a weird one-night stand, she couldn't shake the memory of him flush against her.

"Yes, I'd like that. Say seven?" Maybe she'd stop being such a coward.

"Perfect." Draven went back to work.

Thana and Lola passed through the door into the hallway.

"I don't like him. Something about him is just off," Lola said quietly as they entered the bright and lemon smelling kitchen.

"Give him a chance, please?" Thana asked. She didn't know what else to say. Lola was fearful of every male that stepped onto the property. Thana understood why, but she didn't know how to help. She and Morana were already trying to find a therapist in town for Lola.

"How do you even have time to sleep?" Thana asked as she watched Morana making a lemon tart. Their pantry, fridge, and freezer were stuffed with her baked goods, from sweet to savory. One thing was for sure. They wouldn't starve.

"The workers get hungry," Morana said. She looked tired and there were bags under her eyes. She'd taken to making a few things each day to give to the construction workers.

"You look tired," Lola said.

"Well, if they didn't start working at five a.m., I wouldn't be."

"Five a.m.?" Thana and Lola shared a quizzical glance. "Morana, no one is here that early."

Morana stopped working and frowned at them, "Are you are sure? Every day for a week I've been woken up at five a.m. to banging noises. They quiet down long enough for me to start to fall back to sleep and then start up again. I finally give up and just get up."

"I haven't heard anything," Thana said.

"Me either," Lola agreed.

"Maybe it's the pipes? You are next to the bathroom," Thana suggested.

"Maybe." But she didn't sound convinced.

"I'll ask Dorian about it. I'm sure we can fix it." Thana gave her sister a large reassuring smile.

"Maybe we could leave the house, go into town or on a walk? All this noise and dust is giving me a headache," Lola said. She sat down at the table and instantly Morana put food in front of her. A plate filled with sweet fried plantains. Their sister had lost a good twenty pounds in the last few months and it showed in an unhealthy way.

"Out of the house. But there's so much to do?" Thana watched as a look passed between her sisters. They were hiding something.

"Or we could go for a drive. Find a creek to wade in?" Morana suggested.

"Okay, what's going on?" Thana asked.

Morana gave her a wide-eyed, nothing-why-are-you-asking look.

"Oh, just tell her," Lola said.

Morana's shoulder's sagged. "Trixie sent me an email today."

"And…." Thana was becoming irritated.

"A small story ran about Forgotten Hills reopening," Lola explained.

"Why would that bother…. No…they mentioned the Lottes, didn't they?" Thana sank down in her chair. Great, just what she needed.

"Yeah, they did mention you were not part of the investigation and had nothing but positive reviews from people you worked with, but it rehashed the entire drama and mentioned Dani," Morana said.

"Do you think this will affect Forgotten Hills?" Thana asked, ignoring the rest.

"No, the family has too many ties and too good a reputation. You may want to invite someone out here to do an article on the re-opening though," Lola said.

That was a great suggestion! They'd want a tour though, couldn't do that with the body in the basement. Couldn't tell a journalist she wasn't like the Lottes if she had a random dead woman downstairs.

"How about that walk?" Morana proposed, trying to change the subject, lighten the mood. Thana appreciated it.

"Not in the cemetery, not in the mood." Lola halfheartedly began to pop the sugary plantain bites in her mouth. They were a golden caramel color with a delicious crust.

"We own a few acres next to the crematory, how about that? I think I saw a small path we could follow," Thana said, playing along. She didn't want to think about her past anymore.

"I'll pack us a lunch and we can make an afternoon of it," Morana said.

"I'd like that." Lola ate more of her food, rolling her eyes as Morana set a tall glass of iced tea in front of her with a plate of pink and blue macaroons.

"I saw you sewing this morning. What are you making?" Thana asked, sitting next to her sister and grabbing a cookie. She didn't like macaroons, but it was an act of solidarity.

"A new dress, something cheery," Lola said.

"I like the sound of that. I was getting tired of you wandering the halls in sweatpants and hand me down scrubs." Morana went to the sink and began to clean up. It seemed as if she were done cooking for the day. Dinner must already be in the fridge awaiting the oven.

Lola cracked a smile and a rare burst of laughter slipped from her lips. "Me, too."

Morana and Thana looked at each other, each hoping the same thing. That this was a sign their sister was starting to feel normal again.

"Why don't we all change and meet back here at noon?" Thana asked. Getting an affirmative response, Thana went upstairs.

It was still strange to go into Lorelei's room and see her own things. She still expected her aunt to be sitting in the old rocker and smile at her.

Maybe that was why, over the last few days, she'd started to feel uneasy in the room. It was still a warm comfortable space combining her and Lorelei. However, Thana couldn't shake the feeling she didn't belong there, that sometimes she wasn't alone.

It was ridiculous. Thana did not believe in ghosts and if

she did it should be a comforting thought that Lorelei was checking in on her.

It wasn't comforting; it was the opposite. Forgotten Hills was her new home and she needed the stability of having a permanent location.

While Morana planned on returning to Portland in just a few weeks, this was where Thana wanted to spend the rest of her life. It was where Lola would live until she was well, back on her feet, and had a plan.

"Thana."

Hearing her name Thana turned toward the bedroom door, expecting to see one of her sisters. No one was there. She walked back out into the living room and glanced around, "Lola? Morana?" she called. She could hear the construction, a normal sound, like familiar pressure in her mind. She'd gotten used to the constant hammering and drilling.

"Thana."

Her name again. This time she concentrated. It didn't sound like one of her sisters. It didn't sound like anyone she knew. Going into the study she checked if the computer was on, maybe connected to Skype?

It wasn't and the fact that she was alone upstairs sank in, icy and painful in her chest. It was her imagination. It had to be.

"Thana." This time the voice was coming from inside her bedroom. Fear crept into her veins. Was she losing her mind? Had she finally spent too much time with the dead and not noticed her sanity slip through her fingers?

Taking a few steps toward her door she watched in horror like slow motion as her bedroom door silently swung shut.

A hand touched her shoulder and Thana jumped, apprehension stuck in her throat.

"Geeze, are you ok? What's wrong?" Morana asked, her

head was cocked to one side as she looked worriedly at Thana.

Thana composed herself in less than a second. She took a big calming breath of warm air, relishing in the bright citrus scent that followed Morana from the kitchen.

"Did you call for me?" Thana asked, regulating her breathing.

"I did. Do you think I can wear shorts?" Morana asked.

That must have been it. Morana's voice just traveled strangely up the stairs. Nothing else made sense.

And the door? A little voice in her mind asked. Thana's eyes lingered on her shut bedroom door and a tingle of alarm attached to her spine.

"No, too chilly and I'm not sure the path's condition is great," Thana finally answered her sister.

"Are you okay?" Morana asked.

"Yes, fine. Just preoccupied."

"Well, snap out of it." Morana went into her own room.

Cautiously Thana approached her door, hand shaking as she reached for the knob and threw the door open. It banged against the wall, rattling the wood.

No one was inside, of course not. All that happened was simply like one of Morana's recipes. One old house, a cup of stress, 400 pounds of building equipment. A whiff of Morana's voice and a creepy body in the freezer. Combine, stir and get Thana freaking out over nothing.

Going to her dresser she pulled on copper leggings and a dark blue tunic style knit sweater. She added brown hiking boots and braided her hair.

With a little time to spare, she went to speak to Draven. His eyes widened when he saw her.

"What, what's wrong?" She patted her head and glanced down at her outfit.

"Nothing is wrong. You just look like you," he said.

"I always look like me."

"No, you look like what you think you should look like. Now you look like the girl I met in the cemetery." He relaxed back in his chair. Today he was in a flannel button-up in reds and browns with jeans. When she'd asked him where his suit was, he'd told her he couldn't wear it and help the builders.

Honestly, she liked him better this way. With his silver hair fly away and a teasing and friendly expression in his eyes.

"We're going for a hike in the woods," she said and watched a steel and cool mask settle over his face She'd learned over the past two weeks that it meant she wasn't going to like what he had to say or that he didn't agree with something she was doing. He wouldn't even talk to her about the contents in her aunt's letter.

"That's a bad idea. No one goes in those woods. People get lost and it gets dark quickly. Why do you think your aunt never developed it?"

"Because it's a money pit to try and develop land like that without knowing you can turn a profit from it," Thana answered, hands on her hips.

"No. I wish you'd listen to me."

"I wish you'd actually talk to me. We seem to get along fine and then you say something like this. Something that makes me feel like you're keeping secrets. I never kept secrets from you, Draven, but ever since you walked back into my life, it's all you've done." It was like a double-edged sword. She'd missed him. Wondered where he'd gone and what he was doing. Searched for him on Myspace and then Facebook and Twitter. But without the last name or being able to ask Lorelei, it was all but hopeless and she'd eventually given up.

"I know it's frustrating and all I can say is, I'm sorry." Draven stood and came around the desk, he reached out and took her hand.

His hands felt strong, warm and firm against her skin. He rubbed a spot on her palm. She felt her cheeks flush and fought off a desire to duck her head and stare at her toes.

"I wanted to contact you, but I made a promise to your aunt I wouldn't until she died."

"Why would you agree to that?" The thickness in her voice giving away how she felt. *Ask him about that night, ask him now!* the voice in her head screamed.

Those weird green eyes bore into her and she couldn't read the emotion in them. Her eyes strayed to his mouth and she wondered what it would be like to kiss him again.

"I had to. Thana, don't go into the woods. Stop disturbing what has always been here. You will regret it."

"Did you just fucking threaten my sister?"

Draven dropped her hand like she'd burned him. Sitting on the edge of his desk, he gave Lola a level stare. "I would never do that."

Lola stood, petite and pretty in jeans and white cardigan, looking furious with pink flooding her cheeks and tears in her eyes.

"He wasn't threatening me. There have been some eccentric issues since we got here that Draven is helping with," Thana said, moving to stand in front of her.

"That's not what it sounded like."

"Don't worry about it. Draven is a…friend." Thana looked over her shoulder and watched his shoulders relax. He nodded his head and quickly went back to work.

"Come on, let's go outside and wait for Morana."

EIGHT

WHEN LOLA WAS FIVE, LORELEI STARTED TEACHING HER TO sew. Thana never understood why Lola was so interested in the patterns, the fabric's name or if a certain color matched another color. You went to the store and bought clothes, end of story.

But Lola would watch Lorelei work at her sewing machine for hours, the little machine's rhythm and hum like a never-ending song. Lola ran her hands over the vibrant and eclectic outfits Lorelei created and screamed in glee whenever their aunt made something for them to wear.

Lorelei made bright pink stockings with pigs embroidered on them, long white nightgowns with seashell buttons and colored lace collars, woven belts in wool and hemp.

The first thing Lorelei taught Lola to make was a skirt. Thana remembered how proud she was showing it off, even though the hem wasn't even, and it was too big around the waist. Though she'd admired the pale peach color and how it complimented her sister's skin tone.

Even years after they'd been banished from Forgotten Hills, Lola maintained a passion for making her own clothing.

She made their prom dresses, intricate designs made to draw out their beauty while hiding their birthmarks. She created a floor-length ice blue taffeta princess dress for herself, a long-sleeved bronze silk empress style for Thana and a high collared vintage lace gown for Morana.

There were pale green and blue quilts, snarky embroidered hangings, stitched handkerchiefs and books filled with designs.

Lola was an artist and one day when she was twenty, she drew something different. Not a blazing dress of fire or a coat fit for a prince. No this was something different. She drew Forgotten Hills and she drew it for Thana.

The blue-green twilight cemetery was a gothic fairy tale land next to a rambling house that looked like it was sad and beautiful all at once.

She told Thana she had woken from a dream and had to draw it. She framed it and gave it to her for Christmas.

Thana took it as a sign they would one day be reunited with what the girls considered their "true" home. She just wished it wasn't because their beloved aunt was dead.

———

The path into the forest started off well enough. Since it was almost fall, the foliage was turning brown and orange with a hint of green still struggling among the dirt and leaves that filled the forest floor. The path was packed dirt and overgrown with weeds asserting their dominance.

Tall trees shaded the forest so that only hints of sunlight streamed through. A mix of Dogwood and white oak trees that looked like the gods had spilled red, orange and green paint over them as the seasons changed.

A crisp earthy aroma filled Thana's nose as they stepped onto the path and began their walk. It was chilly, but not uncomfortable. Lola carried a large blue blanket and Morana held a small cooler filled with deviled egg sandwiches, homemade beet chips and a thermos of hot chocolate.

"Oh, this is pretty," Lola sighed, kicking a rock down the tiny path, dirt smearing the toe of her blue tennis shoes.

"Why didn't we ever do this as kids?" Morana asked.

"Why would we when we had Forgotten Hills? It's a sanctuary." Thana had to admit the woodland was pretty, but deep inside she'd rather be doing this in their special spot among the graves.

"That looks like a great spot," Lola said after twenty minutes. She pointed to a flat area surrounded by trees.

"Let's check it out. I don't want a rock up my butt," Morana muttered pushing ahead of them. She stomped around the little clearing and then proclaimed it "suitable."

Lola spread out the blanket and soon they were eating lunch in the cool forest while sparkles of sunshine flitted down around them.

"Do you smell licorice?" Lola asked after eating half her sandwich.

Lifting her head Thana took a deep breath in through her nose, "I guess, under the smell of egg it's kind of there."

"Wild fennel," Morana said around a mouth full of salty crunchy goodness.

"What was that?" Thana asked, laughing.

Morana swallowed. "Wild fennel. It smells like anise or black licorice."

"How do you know that?" Lola asked.

"I cook with it. Locally grown and foraging is the way to live," Morana countered. She pointed at a sad looking plant with yellow flowers a few feet away. "A lot of people like to chew it."

"Gross," Lola said.

"Hey, what's that over there?" Thana asked. She'd noticed something in the distance, something that shouldn't be there.

"Is it a fence?" Morana asked.

"We're still on our property. What would a fence be doing out here?" Thana stood and wiped her hands on her pants. Stepping off the blanket, she made her way over.

"Wait for us!" Lola called and Thana heard her sisters scrambling after her.

Pushing through tall yellow grass, Thana came to a halt in front of a small area of forest that was fenced off. A tiny square around what looked like nothing. The grass inside was just as tall as it was outside.

"Is there a way in? They can't have fenced off nothing," Morana said.

The fencing was old, fifty years or so. Many places were rusted through and sagging, several edges looked jagged enough that the thought of touching them made Thana want to get a tetanus shot.

"Here!" Lola exclaimed. She was toward the back, leaning down and tearing weeds away from a small metal gate. There was a latch that looked older than the gate and it took all three girls pushing together to move it open.

The gate made a screeching noise so high pitched it was painful. It was clear no one had come anywhere near this strange area in decades.

As they crossed into the space, roughly 600 square feet, Thana noticed something was in the very middle and she put a hand out stopping her sisters from going in any further.

"We should leave," she said.

"No way. It's just like when we were kids, discovering, exploring," Lola argued, her face flushed. She was enjoying herself and Thana hated to take that away.

"What's wrong?" Morana asked.

Thana sighed. She couldn't think of a lie convincing

enough to get them to go back to Forgotten Hills. "I think it's a grave."

Both her sisters turned to stare at her.

"What makes you think that?" Morana asked.

"Only you would find an abandoned grave during a picnic," Lola snorted.

"Just…just stay here while I look. If it's historical, I don't want to damage anything," Thana said. Carefully she made her way to the center and there it was.

A faded headstone about a foot high made from a beige stone. Flowers were carved into the stone; poppies, lilies, and daffodils. All symbols for death and eternity in the world of headstone symbolism.

Kneeling, she used her sleeve to clean the front as best she could. She needed to get a good look at the dates to tell if a call to her mother was necessary. If this was Native American, the entire area would need to be investigated.

As the words became clear, Thana's heart beat louder in her ears until the rushing of her own blood drowned out the forest sounds and her sisters questioning voices.

Dabria Muerticillo
04/03/1820-09/18/1845

Beneath it was quite possibly the creepiest epitaph Thana had ever read.

To save us all she took death as a lover.

"You young ladies really shouldn't disturb poor Dabria," a voice called out from the wood. All three women jumped in fright.

"A ghost?" Lola asked, only half joking.

"If ghosts crave licorice roots." An older woman shambled out from the brush. She held a basket filled with wild herbs and plants and her jeans and sweater was covered in weeds and dirt.

Her black skin was smooth with faint signs of aging and she had curly short salt and pepper hair. Jammed onto of her head was a haphazardly placed wide brim straw hat.

She pulled off gardening gloves as she came closer, her eyes bright and her smile wide and friendly.

"Who are you?" Morana asked.

"Lydia Gilhoulie. Your aunt and I have been neighbors our entire lives," she said. She didn't come all the way to the fence line. She glared at the metal wires like it was offensive and kept her distance.

"I think I remember you," Thana said, squinting.

"I often came to give your aunt herbs for her cooking. I collect and grow quite a few. You were all such happy, beautiful girls."

"How do you know about Dabria?" Morana asked.

"The whole town knows about her. I suggest you leave her gravesite alone."

"Wait, who is Dabria?" Lola asked, confusion apparent on her face.

"We'll tell you when we get home," Morana said. Lola opened her mouth to protest and then snapped it shut, crossing her arms under her breasts in a stubborn Lola stance.

"But Dabria isn't buried here," Thana said.

"She was supposed to be. Whether she physically resides beneath that dirt isn't important. It is her grave," Lydia said.

Her aunt's letter hadn't mentioned that Dabria had a grave. Why wouldn't the poor girl have been left to rot in peace?

"We don't like people to come poking around here looking for her. Didn't your aunt tell you?" Lydia asked.

"Who is Dabria? Morana, explain now," Lola said. She grabbed Morana's arm and dragged her from the tiny graveyard toward their forgotten picnic.

"She mentioned it, but this place doesn't look like hordes of visitors tramp through my woods to find it. How would they even know it's here?" Thana asked. In fact, until they stumbled upon it, the grave didn't look like anyone had been near it in years.

"If you search the web long enough you will find pictures and a description of how to get here. The private property warnings don't do much," Lydia explained. "Now come out of there."

Thana bristled. Who was this old woman to tell her what to do?

"We should clean it up and bury her—"

"No! Don't disturb her or her grave. If you know what's good for you, you'll forget you ever saw this place." A storm rolled over Lydia's features and Thana was surprised at how upset she was.

All this time she'd thought Draven was crazy, but maybe it was the whole town.

"You can't honestly believe she saved the town from death all those years ago. She's an innocent woman who deserves a proper burial."

"Suicide prevents a proper burial and you will find the whole town believes it. We are alive today because of Dabria's sacrifice."

"My aunt couldn't have believed this," Thana said. It was nonsense, superstition wrapped around a dead body. A woman who didn't ask to be the star in some twisted legend.

"You'd be surprised what your aunt believed," Lydia said.

Thana didn't want to upset her anymore.

Who knew how her health was? She was obviously not mentally well if she believed a dead body could carry magical powers. Making her way slowly out, she shut the gate behind her. It pained her to leave it in such a state. The fence needed repair, the gate should have a lock and the area needed to be weeded.

She could hear her sisters arguing a few feet away.

"I can't believe you didn't tell me!" Lola exclaimed.

"We didn't want to upset you!" Morana yelled.

"Well, I'm upset now and there is a frozen dead girl in the basement." Lola stomped over to Thana.

"Thana," she said, out of breath, skin pale and eyes wide, "we cannot live with that girl in the basement. If this is her grave, she has to be buried."

"It's a mortuary, there will always be dead people in the basement." Thana tried for logic.

Lola bit her lip and frowned up at her big sister. "That's not the same and you know it. What was Lorelei thinking, leaving us this place with this kind of baggage?"

"She was thinking that the three of you would be able to handle it together," Lydia answered.

"What?" Morana asked, coming to stand next to them. She tried to put an arm around Lola who was trembling as the sun moved and it became late afternoon. A slight wind kicked up, rustling through the tall grass around Dabria's grave.

"She told me that only you girls had what it took to come back here. That you, Thana, were destined to be Dabria's next keeper."

"That is crazy talk, Thana," Lola said. She shivered. "I want to go home."

"Back to New York?" Morana asked, aghast.

"No... No... just back to... Forgotten Hills, I guess," Lola said. She sounded like a little girl, lost.

"It's going to be dark in a few hours. I never stay in the wood this late and you shouldn't either. I'll stop by sometime with some sage cornbread muffins. They were your aunt's favorite." Lydia smiled at them, showing brilliant white teeth.

"Aunt Lorelei was a great cook. Why didn't she make her own?" Morana asked.

"I wouldn't give her my recipe," Lydia said, laughing.

She clutched her basket full of fragrant herbs to her chest and began walking back the way she came. Right before she disappeared into the shady trees, Thana called after her, "Does everyone know this grave is here?"

"Of course," Lydia said, her words floating back to Thana.

"Really? Even Draven?" She couldn't believe he wouldn't have said something, to warn her. Especially since he was on the leave-Dabria-alone bandwagon.

Lydia tossed a curious look over her shoulder pausing mid-step. "Who is Draven?"

NINE

THANA WISHED SHE COULD RELAX AS SHE STEPPED INTO THE cemetery. Her feet sank into the forest green grass and the familiar smells and feelings tried to swallow her. Still, there was this pressure between her shoulder blades; a tightening she could feel in all her skin.

"I say we start here and make the circle," Draven said, pointing at where the official cemetery path started.

"Sounds good," Thana agreed, and they started walking. The path wound around near the outer wall at first before winding toward the center in a swirling pattern. She knew it would end where Elder still sat with his weeping angels. The highest point in the cemetery.

A very faint wind rattled the leaves and branches and she could hear sounds coming from the house as well as birds and the general music of the outdoors.

They walked in silence, keeping their distance. It was almost uncomfortable, and Thana wished she'd never agreed to this outing. She felt grumpy and agitated, tense.

After walking in silence in the lush childhood playground, her heart wouldn't let her hold on to her annoyance. The headstones were beige, white, gray and brown against the overtly green background. It was the same and yet so much different than it had been. Now she could see the ravages of time, from broken and chipped marble to trees and plants that needed a gardener's care.

The beauty was still there too. She saw flowing vines and plants struggling to produce flowers against the oncoming cold. She saw lamb statues on children's headstones and the solemn faces of a dozen carved angels. Hills hid elaborate monuments with book long epitaphs; everything ripe with history, begging not to be forgotten.

As they came around one hill there it was: the ring. Just like she remembered. The wall here was lower, part of it crumbled at the base, as it always had been. As her eyes strayed to the dates and she realized they all died a day before Dabria.

It was then she noticed the silence. No air moved in this space, there was no noise, like this little circle of nameless tombstones lay in a void.

"I thought since you had workers here already, they could fix this spot in the wall, as much as it is a fond memory for me," Draven said, as they paused their walk.

"Yeah, sure…" Thana said, preoccupied. She felt like she was being watched. An unpleasant tingling sensation was creeping up her spine until the hairs on the back of her neck stood up with electricity.

Rubbing her neck, she looked around; was there a visitor in the cemetery?

"Why don't they have names? I assume they are all plague victims," Thana said, stiffly, making her way into the center of the ring.

"I don't know. You are correct they are plague victims, but I don't know why they have no names. There might be records in your aunt's things somewhere," Draven said.

"Do you feel that?" she asked as the sensation of being watched changed into the knowledge that she wasn't welcome in this circle; how had she eaten lunch here as a child? It made her stomach queasy and her mind afraid.

"It's always colder over here than everywhere else," Draven said. She noticed he circled the ring but wouldn't come in to meet her.

"Remember the first time we met?" he asked.

"How could I forget you? You were just this strange boy sitting on the wall. You're still a strange boy." Thana forced a smile and moved from the center, but still within the ring. Instantly the uncomfortable feelings diminished, they didn't vanish, but they were tolerable.

Mine. She heard the voice, it was just a whisper on the air, but it sounded angry and possessive.

"Did you hear that?" she asked. Draven didn't acknowledge her. He kept looking at the wall.

"You were such a small thing, but all fury and strength. You'd rushed into the ring angry after speaking to your mother," Draven said.

"I know. I was about to have a good angry cry when I heard you. I was startled, thought you were a ghost," Thana said, frowning at him. What did that matter now?

"Once you realized I wasn't the undead, you asked me if I was okay. You who were hurt, thought of me first. I hadn't known kindness like that in…well a long time." He turned to face her, and she took a step back, banging the back of her knees into marble. Something in his eyes was hungry, some twisted motive swirled deep in those off green depths. She tried to focus on it, but it was gone. This place was playing havoc with her senses.

Mine, leave now. She heard the voice again, turning her head in every direction she tried to figure out where it was coming from.

"Come on, you had to have heard that."

Again, he ignored her. "No one has been my friend since you, Thana, even your aunt kept me at a distance."

"Draven, why are you saying all of this? When I first arrived, you acted like we were strangers. It really hurt. You were my first friend outside of my sisters. I honestly figured I'd imagined it all." Thana was defensive and frustrated. Draven's mood was like the weather.

"I'm sorry. I had to make sure you were planning to stay, and I need you to leave Dabria alone. You have to understand the whole town will suffer if you disturb her."

"I am staying. I don't know about my sisters, but this is my home now." At least she thought it was. The intense feeling of being unwanted was wrapping around her so she couldn't focus. Every inch of her skin was covered in goosebumps like a malevolent presence was drilling holes into her back with its gaze.

"And how could an entire town suffer from disturbing one dead woman?"

"Can't you ever just believe me?" he asked quietly.

"No. The last time I did that you told my aunt nothing we'd talked about was significant." She hurled the words to be hurtful and it worked. He winced.

"You know I only said that so she wouldn't know the truth."

"Why would that have mattered?"

"It just would."

She was done with this line of conversation. It was a game and it made her head hurt.

"I found her grave in the woods," Thana said. "She needs to be buried. I don't know what kind of crazy superstitions you and the people of this town believe, but it's beyond disrespectful for her body to spend eternity in a freezer."

Go NOW! the voice shouted, and Thana jumped, startled.

Draven reached into the circle and took her arm pulling her out.

"I will try and protect you if you let me," Draven said, leading her away from the ring, following the back wall near where many members of her family were buried. Grandparents, great grandparents, a few great uncles and aunts, some fourth, fifth and sixth cousins. Just a ton of her family that stayed in Forgotten Hills.

"Protect me? From what? Crazy town people, a frozen girl in the basement, death?"

Draven gave a low chuckle. "Sadly, I cannot protect you from death."

He took that moment to slip his hand into hers. A burning cold ran from his fingers to *it* and Thana didn't know if she wanted to pull back or take his other hand for more contact.

"What are you doing?" she asked. He'd made it clear these past few weeks that he was interested in a friendly working business relationship, but not in rekindling the same relationship they'd had in the past.

"This place, makes me think, makes me want things I cannot have, not yet," he said, lips turning into a grimace, eyes bright.

"You were always a strange kid, Draven, but you've become an even weirder adult," Thana told him. She needed to ask him…now.

"So, you saw her grave in the woods?" he asked.

"You knew it was there? Why didn't you tell me?"

"Something you needed to see for yourself. You need all the pieces to be successful and I am forbidden from helping you."

"Stop being so damn cryptic. It's not cute or sexy. It's annoying as hell!" she exclaimed. She tried to pull away, but he wouldn't let her. Instead he pulled her closer to him. She could smell the forest like cologne he wore, and she really liked it, maybe too much.

"I'm sorry, but you cannot bury Dabria, you must continue to be her keeper."

"Until I die? Then I pass on this job to one of my children or nieces?"

"Yes."

He let go of her hands and touched her shoulders, turning her from him.

She saw it instantly.

There, nearest the path, bright and shining was a new headstone with her aunt's name and information.

"I thought mom said they didn't bury her here. We would have come to the funeral!" Thana exclaimed. She walked quickly to her aunt's grave and knelt in front of it, her hands planted in the cold thick grass, slight moisture leaking through the knees of her leggings.

"Yes, half the town attended. I'm sorry your mother lied."

"Lorelei was more of a mother than mine was and I lost her the year I was fifteen. This just makes it permanent," Thana said, a tear slipped down her face and she furiously brushed it away. Little traitor. Thana didn't cry.

Thana traced the numbers of birth and death with her finger, taking a deep breath in to stop a sob.

"The Death Keeper?" She read out loud the words under the dates. "What kind of epitaph is that?"

"Traditional," Draven said. He was standing next to her and all she could see were his pants and shoes.

Rocking back on her heels she looked to where he was pointing, half of all the graves buried near her aunt had the same sentence engraved on them.

She stood and shakily made her way through the headstones and dotted between normal phrases like "Beloved

Father" "Gone but not Forgotten" "Till We Meet Again," and "Greatly loved" were a dozen that read, "The Death Keeper."

"Is this my fate?" she asked.

"Yes. I wish I could change it for you," Draven whispered. He was standing so close to her.

"Was my aunt happy?" Thana asked, but she knew the answer to the question.

"Yes. She told me she loved only one thing more than all of Forgotten Hills." Draven linked his fingers through hers again.

"What was it?"

She turned her face up to his and right before his lips descended onto hers, he whispered, "You."

Just that word and his lips sent Thana's world spinning out of control. His mouth on hers was fire and ice. She wanted to dive into the feelings and never return, but she knew she had to ask him.

She pushed him away, he looked shocked.

"I have to know something, Draven." She was so nervous. What if he told her he didn't know what she was talking about?

He took a step closer to her, his hand on her waist he leaned in, staring into her eyes. "Yes."

"Yes, what?" It was hard to form words.

"I was there that night, with you."

Heart skipping, she tried to make sense of his words. "Why did you leave without saying anything to me?" How had he known what she was going to ask?

For the first time in her memory, he blushed. "I woke up and panicked. I decided last minute to come see you. I overheard Lorelei and your mother talking on the phone, and before I knew it, I was in my car. I almost turned around a dozen times. I stood outside that door for five minutes debating with myself. I just wanted to congratulate you, to see you again. Then you answered the door in your underwear, and I couldn't think, let alone make a moral decision."

"Moral?" she asked.

"Thana." He ran a hand through his hair, and added, "You were so drunk, in no way could you consent. I felt like an ass. I thought the last thing you'd want was to see me when you woke. And it wasn't like we could be together, things were still, are still, so complicated. I only wanted to see you."

"You are an idiot," Thana said. It appeared to be the last thing he expected her to say.

"I wanted you to be there when I woke up, I was heartbroken when you weren't. Thought I'd drunk-dreamed it all, or worse, taken a stranger home with me and imagined he was you." Reaching up she put her hands on either side of his face. What was she doing? She never acted like this, but something about the cemetery made a reckless urge flutter under her collarbone, a feeling deep within her like she was craving something she couldn't put her finger on.

She kissed him. She kissed him like she hadn't kissed anyone but him in the past twenty years. Not even Dani. Nothing had ever come close to feeling like this.

Draven gripped her and where his hands touched her, she burned. She threw caution to the wind and didn't stop his hands as they roamed over her. She helped him take off her leggings and panties. She begged him to touch her and relished in the way he said her name, telling her that he'd never wanted anyone as he wanted her.

It couldn't have taken more than a few minutes. All she could see was him and the green of the cemetery and all she could feel was pleasure bubbling in her veins. The cool grass on her skin sent shivers all over her and his weight on top of her was familiar and comforting.

When he slid inside her she cried out at the full and heavy sensation; intense and erotic. He fucked her there, surrounded by the dead. It was fast, hard and hot. Her breath left her lungs and didn't come back until the pain-pleasure line burst and she came, tightening around him. He growled her name as he spilled hot seed inside of her, taking her mouth with his, fingers digging into her shoulders as their bodies stilled and cooled.

As they lay together catching their breath, reason and common sense flooded through her and she pushed him away, scrambling for her clothes even as evidence of their time together trickled down her leg. What had she done? There was too much to do for her to have a romantic entanglement right now. She didn't make decisions on a whim. She needed to weigh the pros and cons. They hadn't even used protection!

"This isn't me," she said, struggling into clothes. He didn't look at her, he simply rolled onto his back, naked and unashamed staring at the sky.

"This is you, you hide behind rational overthinking, Thana, when really you're like Lorelei; passionate and wild," he said. "Come back to me."

"I don't know if we should do that again."

"We've done it before and be certain we will again," he said.

"Wow, that was very…unattractive and cocky." The need to push him away was in a battle with wanting him never to leave her side.

"I know, and I'm sorry. It was wonderful, Thana. Thank you." He looked at her and she couldn't look away. She wanted to get down on the ground with him and run her hands all over his skin. To spend hours talking to him and getting to know him all over again. Sex would just be a bonus. But they weren't children anymore. She hadn't been for several decades, and with that came responsibility and having sex with Draven in a cemetery wasn't responsible or safe.

"What if I'm pregnant? We didn't use protection!" She ran hands over her face, irritated.

"It cannot happen, don't worry about that. Nor do you need to worry about diseases." He stood and began to dress.

"So, you're sterile?" Why the thought made her sad she didn't know.

Draven thought for a moment and nodded in confirmation.

"I want you again, Thana. I hope you favor a reoccurrence."

"Favor a reoccurrence? Who says that?" Did he want to be her boyfriend now? No…that's not what he'd said. He just wanted to fuck her again. Thana stopped to consider, even as the air around them grew into night and the cold seeped through her sweater. Would that be so bad? A friend with benefits situation when the sex was literally the best she'd ever had?

"Let me think about it. God, this has been a crazy damn day," Thana said, "and you are a study in contradictions."

"I don't just want sex, Thana, but I will take whatever you are comfortable with. Do you want me to come back inside with you?" He held out his hand and smiled at her and it was full of warmth and promise, but a sadness she didn't understand lurked in his eyes.

"No, not tonight. I have to shower and talk to my sisters."

"Then we should both go. This is not a place to be at night." Draven motioned to the deepening shadows and Thana agreed with him. Her aunt hadn't allowed them to play in the cemetery at night. In fact, she hadn't liked to let them wander outside much at all after dark.

Morana, Lola, and Thana had always considered it one of her weird quirks without reason.

As Thana made her way back to the house she thought about the voice. Maybe her aunt had a good reason after all.

TEN

Summers Past

THEIR MOM AND DAD NEVER DROVE THEM TO OREGON. THEY never took a family trip in a car, dozens of hours together, playing games, eating crappy food. Thana and her sisters smooshed together in the back seat fighting over space, legs sticking together.

They never saw what lay between their home in Arizona and Oregon from the seats of their station wagon. They didn't travel the long highway with nothing but desert as far as the eye could see, or the winding freeway curving up the California coast.

Instead, they memorized airport layouts. When they were too young to travel unaccompanied, mom and dad would schedule a layover in Portland so that Lorelei could pick them up and then they'd zoom off to whatever foreign destination awaited. As they got older, they made up games to play as they sat in the Phoenix airport and watched all the different people come and go. They charmed flight attendants into giving them extra snacks and chatted up old ladies who smelled of peppermint.

Getting off the plane in Oregon was like a breath of fresh air. Lola oversaw Morana while Thana got their bags. Three matching blue suitcases that took all the coordination in her young arms to maneuver and balance.

They would wind and weave through throngs of people, most who didn't pay attention to the three little girls deftly making their way outside.

Once outside, they always stood in the same place and waited. Sometimes they waited in the chilly air, goosebumps forming on bare legs, thin arms wrapped around each other for warmth. Other times they huddled under a large green umbrella while wind and rain whipped around them.

If they were lucky, the weather was mild and they could sit, backs against the wall and share the sandwiches mom packed, discussing what sort of adventure the summer would bring. Thana remembered the way the tangy mustard and cheese tasted against the dry bread, a bottle of water passed back and forth with tiny food particles floating in it.

Sometimes people stopped and asked them if they needed help, but mainly they were ignored.

Then right as they were about to scrounge up change for a phone call, they would see it, Lorelei's truck. Rust colored and large with her smiling behind the wheel. She'd pull up next to them, park and lean over, throwing the door wide. Morana and Lola would scramble in next to her while Thana threw their bags in the back.

It took three hours to get to Hill City from the airport, but the trip always ended up being closer to five.

Lorelei took back roads, showing them great green expanses of forest that smelled sweet and wet. She pulled over so they could dangle feet in creeks or skip rocks across the water. She bought honey and jerky from roadside stands and fed them pancakes at whatever diner was closest to the road.

They visited every museum from Hill City to Portland, they'd seen old graveyards, historical monuments and gotten soaked checking out abandoned buildings.

Lorelei always bought them something; bags of candy, ornaments, hand-sewn scarves or hats. By the time they got to Forgotten Hills, they were exhausted and often dirty. She'd bustle them off into the bath and then comb their hair while she told stories.

She liked telling stories. Thana inherited that talent. She made up tales for them long after they stopped visiting Forgotten Hills. It helped keep them all sane.

———

"Something keeps pinching me," Lola said.

They were sitting on the couch together, watching TV. It was a lazy Sunday, Thana's favorite kind. The sound of rain hitting the roof in a familiar pattern, gray storm clouds as far as the eye could see.

The rain came in steady waves over the past day, which meant no work could be done on the mortuary. So, the sisters decided to grab a pizza and some beer in town and hunker down with TV and junk food.

Thana hadn't told them about what happened with Draven in the cemetery. She wasn't sure herself what happened. She knew she enjoyed it, that she wanted to do it again. Boy did she want to. She was nervous and apprehensive, and those feelings made her avoid Draven over the last couple of days.

"Like, right now? Is it the couch, maybe we should buy a new one?" Morana asked, shifting to look at Lola.

"No, not the couch. At night, while I'm asleep." Lola tucked her knees up to her chin.

"Like a bug? Should we call the exterminator?" Thana asked, taking the remote and hitting mute.

"Like a person." Lola stuck out her arm and shoved the bright blue cashmere sweater as far up as it could go. All over her arm were what looked like little finger pad shaped bruises.

"What the hell?" Morana asked as she leaned down, lightly running a finger over Lola's skin.

"How long has this been going on?" Thana asked.

Lola shrugged, pulling away from Morana and lowering her shirt, "A few days."

"Why didn't you tell us sooner?" Morana looked at Thana over their sister's head, worry in her features and voice.

"I didn't think it was a big deal, until this morning when the pain woke me up. Even then it didn't hurt that badly, just annoying really. Other things hurt worse."

"Maybe it's the bed or your sheets. We'll look tonight and make sure nothing's sticking you or anything," Morana said.

"Yeah, I guess. Should I ask the doctor when I go on Monday?"

They'd found a female doctor in town who had experience dealing with abused women for Lola to see as she healed from her various injuries. Thana was proud of her sister. Lola seemed to be getting stronger, her old personality leaking back into her a day at a time. She'd bought new clothes and had gone back to working at her sewing machine a few hours each day. The east wall of her room was filled with painted flowers and sunshine; a mural she'd taken on to cheer herself up and make sure she didn't "sit in the silence of her mind" too long.

"I think that's a good idea," Thana said.

"Okay, anyone want anything? I'm going downstairs to get a soda." Lola stood up and smiled down at them.

"Sure, bring back some of the caramel popcorn I made today," Morana said.

"And beer!" Thana yelled after her as Lola turned and left.

"Whatcha thinking?" Morana asked as soon as Lola descended the stairs.

"I think she's doing it to herself, subconsciously. Hopefully, her new doctor can help sort it out. Or recommend a therapist who can." Thana sat back and hit the volume button.

The announcer's voice filled the living room announcing the basket ingredients for the dessert round were: fruit punch concentrate, bacon, Peruvian ground cherries, and matcha salt.

"Oooh," Morana leaned forward. "I've never worked with ground cherries."

"What the fuck is a Peruvian ground cherry? Looks like an orange tomatillo."

"Good guess. It's like a tomatillo and a gooseberry had a baby," Morana explained.

"I have no idea what I'd do with that hot mess, make ice cream?"

Morana stared at her like she'd grown another head. Right as she was about to tell Thana the proper way to use the strange ingredients a scream came from downstairs, followed by a crash.

It was breathy and full of terror, and it was Lola's.

Both women jumped off the couch and dashed to the stairs, Morana taking them two at a time allowing her to reach Lola first.

Their sister stood near the dining room table, facing the dark expanse that led down to the prep room. A can of cherry cola lay at her feet, open and fizzing, spilling sticky red liquid over the floor, coming close to Lola's bare toes.

A bowl of caramel popcorn was forgotten on the table next to her. Lola, pale and eyes wide just stood, gripping the edges of her sweater.

"What? What's wrong? Are you okay?" Morana asked, putting an arm around her.

Thana grabbed some paper towels and bent down, cleaning up the mess.

"I thought," Lola gasped, shivering. "I thought I saw... that I..." She blinked a few times and took a deep breath.

"It's silly, but I thought I saw a girl, standing in the stairwell."

"A girl?" Morana looked at Thana. "Do you think someone from the construction crew came in anyway, to do work downstairs?"

"The front and back doors are locked. I wasn't told anyone was coming in. Draven's not even here today." Thana finished cleaning, and straightened, throwing the paper towels into the bin.

"C'mon Lola, you must have imagined it," Morana said. She looked everywhere except the dark.

"I know, but for a second it looked real. Sorry, I scared you. So stupid. Forget I said anything, okay?"

"Yeah, okay, I'll try," Morana mumbled. "Creepy shit sucks."

Thana went over to the dark landing that led down into the basement. A fissure of fear crawled down her spine for a second as she considered the dark. Maybe she'd eat the electricity cost and keep a light on down there. She flipped the switch on the wall and bright florescent light filled the stairway and corresponding lights lit up the basement. The light chased the fear from her. She jogged down the steps and looked around her prep room. No one was there. She checked the outer door and it was locked. The quiet room was unnerving and while she didn't see anything, the room felt like it was...occupied.

The morgue was locked too. She kept the key upstairs in her room. Something she'd never thought to do before until she found the girl in the freezer. As she went back up the stairs, the feeling of not being alone didn't leave. Her hand hovered on the light switch for a second and she decided to leave the lights on.

"It's all good. I think it must have been a trick of the light or your imagination," Thana said.

"I want to go to bed," Lola said.

"Okay, I'll help you." Morana looked confused and Thana knew that boded ill. Morana got testy if something confused her and even crankier if she were frightened.

"I'm going to check the rest of the house. Be right back," Thana said, moving to the door that led to the mortuary.

"Okay, I'll take Lola upstairs. Be careful."

Thana wasn't worried. She knew all the doors were locked and they'd had an alarm system installed at Dorian's insistence. She also knew she wouldn't sleep well if she didn't check, just in case. No one wants to be murdered in their bed because they assumed safety.

It took less than ten minutes for Thana to check every room in the mortuary. Everything was fine, if not a bit spooky. Dim floor lighting lit her path, illuminating enough to see by, but casting ominous shadows. It was silent and unused. Everything simply in stasis, waiting to be important again, to be in use.

"Maybe a lamp will turn on and start singing," Thana said. She turned on every light. Checked every door and window, each cupboard, even the bathroom. Everything was as it should be. Closed and locked, ready for when it was needed.

"Okay," she said to herself as she crossed the reception area again, going back to the kitchen, "9 o clock and all's well." She giggled, then heard a thump from behind her, from a room she'd just been in and time froze. She held her breath, standing still. She stayed as quiet as possible, straining to hear if any more sounds followed.

If this were a horror movie, what would you do? Her inner monologue asked. Simple answer. Don't just stand there. Get back into the bright kitchen and lock the door between you and the noise.

She forced herself to move through the dark and quiet, refusing to look back. Thana made it to the hallway and burst into the kitchen. She slid the old lock on the door and stood, inches from the wood, lights on all around her, staring, waiting.

"You are being ridiculous. Get a grip. There's no one in there, ghosts are not real, and you are not afraid of the dark."

Her pep talk helped her racing heart slow down. She laughed, feeling foolish. If either of her sisters witnessed her acting like a loon she'd never hear the end of it.

It was simply a weird house noise like all houses.

Sitting down at the table Thana absentmindedly began eating popcorn, the golden caramel sticking to her teeth in a salty-sweet rush. Morana always said air popped was the only way to go.

Her pocket buzzed, startling her. Fishing out her cell phone she swiped a finger across the screen to find a text.

LEAVE

She didn't recognize the number. It looked local but didn't appear in her contact list. She fired off a nasty response and hit send. Immediately an error came back saying that her message was undeliverable.

"What the fuck?" she whispered. Was someone in town trying to scare them off? Anger flickered deep in her chest. If that were the case, they would be surprised. It took a lot to truly frighten her and it would take more than spooky old tales and menacing text messages to make her leave Forgotten Hills.

Her eyes focused on the door. Did this text mean the noise she heard was more sinister than she assumed?

Shaking her head, she put her phone away. Nope, now was not the time for flights of fancy and conspiracy theories. It was the time for another beer and bed.

"She's taken a sedative and gone to bed," Morana said as she came back down the stairs. Opening the fridge, she tossed a beer at Thana who caught it with ease. The cold white and blue can numbed her hand. She put it down and relished in the sound it made as she popped the tab.

For a few minutes, Thana and her sister drank in silence. The tangy bubbly liquid went down with a slight burn that was familiar and appreciated. Thana gulped half the can before either of them stopped to speak.

"Man, I hope it was her imagination. I cannot stay here if there's a ghost," Morana said, breaking the silence.

"Morana, there is no such thing as ghosts."

"There better not be or I will flip my shit."

"Of course you will." Thana knew she would; Morana was a big ole scaredy cat. Thana was surprised Lola had seemed so scared, and Lola didn't frighten easily.

"I think we should get that girl out of the basement," Morana said, wiping her mouth on the back of her hand.

"You think knowing she's down there is giving Lola nightmares?" It was something that had already crossed Thana's mind.

"Yeah, like the doctor said. Abused women sometimes suffer from PTSD."

"I'm all for helping her any way we can, but if this one body disturbs her so much, she won't be able to live here when it's a running business."

"I think she'll be fine when it's customers, but this is mysterious, creepy bull shit. Better to be safe than sorry," Morana said. She finished her drink and grabbed the bowl. "Come on. I missed the end of the last episode and another just started. The appetizer round has crickets in it!"

ELEVEN

"TELL US A STORY, LORELEI," LOLA ASKED, SNUGGLED UP next to their aunt. They were laying on a large old blue blanket near the back door. It was a warm but gray day. The sun played hide and seek with the dark clouds that occasionally dropped fat water babies on their heads. Then the warm wind would dry them off as shadows splayed across their skin.

Morana sat at the blanket's edge, painting her toes bright pink, not caring that she was smudging the wet paint with grass, while Thana flipped through the pages of a worn romance novel. She'd already read it twice, but there's only so much room in a suitcase for books when you'll be gone for months.

Morana looked up at their aunt, pausing with the brush against one brown toe. "Oh yes, tell us a story."

"A scary one." Thana grinned, closing her book.

Morana shivered. She was seven and afraid of the dark.

"I don't think Morana would like that," Lola argued. "Tell us a sad story."

"What if I told you one that was a little bit of both?" their aunt asked. She was still lying on her back, eyes closed, ankles crossed wearing green knit booties, hands resting on her round stomach.

"Sounds good," Thana said, book forgotten. Lorelei told the best stories. Thana could never tell if they were true or not. Sometimes she felt as if Lorelei mixed reality and fantasy.

"Once upon a time," Lorelei began.

"Ugh," Thana said.

"In a time long, long ago?" Lorelei peeked at her niece, opening one eye.

"Better."

"There lived a widow who was beloved by all who knew her. She was beautiful, sweet, kind and selfless. She baked bread for the poor, taught Sunday School at church, made dinners for new moms, made sure her house was tidy and her children polite."

"Sounds boring," Morana sighed, toes forgotten.

"To us, maybe. But to her, life was perfect."

"Until…." Lola giggled.

"Until a stranger came to town. He was very handsome, and he brought with him a small caravan full of strange wonders. Things their tiny town had heard about but never seen. Gas lamps, bicycles, exotic cloth, and fancy tools. He brought spices from other countries like curry and saffron. Some foods he peddled the people never dreamed existed. All these things he offered for free on one condition. He be invited into their homes to stay one night and share dinner and breakfast. The widow warned against this as she knew many people did not have food or warmth to spare. She was ignored."

"Weird," Lola said.

"The people were desperate to have these new items. They knew even if they went to larger cities, they could never afford such luxuries. Plus, he was very charming. Soon every family in the village were outdoing themselves to present a welcoming bed and delicious food."

"What kind of things did they serve him?" Morana asked.

"Meat pies, pastries, custard, puddings, whole roast goose, homemade jam, the healthiest, best-tasting vegetables, stews made from prize animals, cakes created with a whole morning's collection of eggs, the sweetest creams, and hand-squeezed juice. Spirits usually saved for holidays were brought out and he slept in the finest bedding the family had, in the biggest bedroom.

"He was there for a month and then as quickly as he came, he left. Within a week of his departure, an evil swept through the town. Children were affected first with rashes and open sores, wet cough, and high fever. Then the elderly got sick until it finally descended upon every single citizen."

"He got them all sick?" Thana asked.

"That's what they assumed. Some people recovered, but many died; small babies, grandparents, fathers, mothers, brothers, and sisters. A quarter of the town dead in three months. The people prayed, they begged, they tried everything they knew about healing. No doctor would come from out of town, in fear of catching the disease and the doctor in town soon ran out of medicine and ideas. In desperation the people held a giant bonfire, burning everything the man had given them, hoping for the best."

"What about the widow?" Lola asked. She was looking confused and anxious. This was a little darker than the tales their aunt normally spun for them.

"While the widow had not wanted anything from the man and had never invited him into her home, the disease was contagious and her youngest child, only three months old, got sick and died. She grieved and decided she would do whatever was necessary to rid her village of disease.

"When another stranger arrived, they were all very wary of him and tried to force him out of town. He told them it was his brother who visited them and made them sick. The town's men tied him up, preparing to punish him for his brother's action. The widow, however, could see how sad and sorry he was. She stopped them from beating him and asked him the question no one else had, can you guess what it was?"

"Why are you here?" Thana guessed; it was the only thing she could think of. Lorelei opened both eyes and turned her head, and smiled at Thana, a soft sad smile.

"Yes, and the man told her he could help. He could cure all who were sick and bring back all those who died. The people did not believe him, but something in his voice made the widow think he was telling the truth and she wanted her baby back. She said she would do anything he asked. She made them untie him with the promise that he would die if he were lying to them."

"Of course, he was, you can't bring the dead back to life," Thana said.

"Zombies," Morana pointed out.

"She took him home and he told her that for all the lives he was saving, he would need one in return, hers. She was afraid at first and upset. If she was dead, who would take care of her baby and her other children? He told her they would be looked after and cared for, forever, so the widow agreed. They spent the entire day and night together."

"Sex," Thana hissed at Lola, who blushed.

"What's sex?" Morana asked.

"Never mind," Lorelei said, frowning at the older two.

"The next morning, he left the house for a few hours and when he came back, he was holding her baby, who looked healthy, strong and alive. The widow cried, gathering the tiny babe to her chest. He said, 'It's time,' and she gave the baby to her oldest daughter and then the widow took the man back into the bedroom. An hour later the daughter went to check on her mother and found her dead, with death's mark on her body. The man was standing next to her, stroking her hair. He told the daughter she must be kept frozen and never buried, never disturbed or the disease would be back."

Lorelei sat up then and turned serious eyes on her audience.

"He told her, 'this above all else; she can never wake, not in spirit, not in flesh, keep her safe and asleep.'

The daughter nodded, though she could tell her mother was dead, not asleep and was feeling all the shock and grief a daughter should feel when discovering her mother dead. She was still holding her baby brother and the man looked down at him. 'He is now touched by death,' he said, 'as is your whole family and town, but you will be alive and healthy.' He left town that night, leaving behind tears of joy and cries of happiness as the sickness lifted and the dead drew in deep breaths and were reunited with loved ones."

"And the baby?" Morana asked.

"Grew up strong and his sister cared for him as her own. The only sign that death had touched him was a round red mark in the middle of his forehead," she ended the story. Each girl staring at her in awe.

"A red mark? Like ours?" Morana asked and Lorelei nodded.

"You should write your stories down and publish a book," Lola said. She grinned and got comfortable, closing her eyes, right as the rain began to fall, its specific smell filling the graveyard.

"Maybe I will. Did you enjoy it, Thana?" Lorelei asked.

"Yes," Thana said. What she didn't say was that it was awfully nice of her aunt to try and give them an origin story that gave meaning to their birthmark. But that's all it was, a story. *It* was nothing but a blemish they were born with, marking them as different and weird.

———

Thana startled awake and took a deep breath, shivering, her dream still resonated clear and in color. She'd forgotten that tale. Not surprising as she had been fourteen with other things on her mind.

Maybe the stories Lorelei told weren't only stories. Maybe hidden in all the nonsense, like people being brought back from the dead, were sparks of truth, things Lorelei had wanted them to know. Things about their family, Forgotten Hills and Hill City. She wondered if her aunt had taken Lola's advice and written them down?

Thana shivered again, drawing her blanket up tighter and noticed she could see her breath like little puffs of smoke. It couldn't possibly be that cold outside? It didn't get to below freezing temperatures in Oregon.

"Thana?" There was a knock on her door, hesitant. "Are you awake?" Lola's voice floated through the wood.

"Yeah, come in." Thana sat up, another shiver rolling down her spine.

The door opened, and both her sisters were there. Morana in a peach robe with thick socks on, carrying a quilted blanket and Lola in a long nightgown and slippers with a buttery yellow shawl over her shoulders.

"It's freezing. Why is it so cold?" Morana asked, rubbing her hands together.

"No idea. Did the furnace stop working?"

"I checked. Says it's set to 68 degrees. Maybe clogged vents?" Lola asked.

"I checked the windows in case one was open or broken

but, as weird as it sounds, I think it's colder in here than it is outside," Morana told her.

Thana got up, grimacing as her bare feet hit the cold wood floor. She was in a tank top and panties and never had she wished more that she liked wearing pants to bed. Rushing to her chest of drawers, fingers freezing she pulled out an oversized sweatshirt and tugged it over her head, grabbing matching sweatpants. The soft thick cotton was a relief on her trembling legs.

Over her sisters' shoulders she could see the light in the living room on, so she knew the electricity was working.

"There's an electric blanket in the closet. Grab it and get in." She pointed to the king-sized bed she'd just crawled out of.

"I'll grab our comforters too. What are you going to do?" Morana asked as Lola hurried to the closet.

"I'm going to check, see if it's cold everywhere, and I'll send a text to Dorian to have him check the insulation and get someone over here to look at the furnace and air vents asap." Thana pulled on socks and her tennis shoes, grabbed her phone and left the room.

Wrapping her arms around herself she went down into the kitchen. It was just as cold, the windows had frost on them. How the hell was that even possible? Maybe the AC was on?

She checked the windows and made sure the thermostat wasn't turned down to freezing. Everything was normal. The gauge was set at the normal 68 degrees and the fan was off.

Each window was shut, and the door closed and locked. Cold and fear radiated within her chest. This couldn't be natural and if it was, her mind couldn't think of one realistic reason, not one idea of what could be causing her home to look like the inside of an iceberg. Leaning over the sink she ran her finger through the flowery ice spirals on the window's ledge, leaving a wet trail as her body warmth melted the ice.

Outside looked cold and wet, but not icy, not freezing. Just a steady downpour of Oregon rain. Large raindrops the definition of wet splashed against grass, trees, and bushes, sending a steady sound through the ceiling and walls into the house. It was a familiar sound.

Thana took a steadying breath and turned. She'd check every room in the entire place and then go back up to her sisters. Pulling out her phone, she opened the camera and took some pictures, sending them and a text to Dorian.

Wait….

Thana squinted in the dark, the only illumination coming from the light she left on in the basement. That bright light leaked into the kitchen allowing her to clearly see that a line of frost was creeping up the stairs.

TWELVE

"What the hell?" Thana asked, her fingers tightened around her phone.

Could the cold be coming from downstairs? Was it possible she left the freezer open? And even if she had, was it conceivable it would flood all Forgotten Hills with the cold?

She ran back upstairs, ignoring her sister's squeaks of protest. She grabbed the key to the morgue and flew back down the stairs. Heart thudding in her chest. She skidded to a halt at the entrance to her prep room.

She began a careful descent down. Each step was icy and the last thing she needed was to fall.

As her prep room and the morgue came into view, she saw everything was covered in a thin film of ice.

"Shit." Now she'd have to check if anything was ruined. Her nose was running, the tip cold. She wiped it on the back of her hand, eyes focused on the freezer. The large door was open. A gaping entryway into a dark box. Why wasn't the interior light on? It should come on if the door is open.

How did the door get open?

She wished Draven was there, had a split-second thought

to go back upstairs and call him and make him check everything out with her. Which was ridiculous. She'd always taken care of everything herself. She never needed anyone but her sisters and even then, she was the one they came to when things needed fixing. She didn't need anyone to help her. No matter if that anyone was handsome and just the thought of sex with him again made her grin and blush.

No, she had to do this…alone.

Picking up speed, her only thought was to get the damn door closed, go back upstairs and get warm. Something inside her mind was screaming at her that she didn't want to see what was in the morgue, even as her mind argued; nothing but metal boxes and space.

She's in there. Whispered her subconscious. *Maybe she's awake.*

The dream, that damned dream was screwing with her head. It was a scary story, that was all. Thana reached the door, gripped the handle and tried to make herself investigate the morgue. She'd need to go in there and find out if the light was broken so she might as well do it now.

She couldn't get her head to turn. All she could make out was a black hole that freezing air was spilling out of.

Just then thunder broke from overhead. With a small cry she slammed the door shut, locked it and ran from the room and back up the stairs, slipping and almost falling as she went. Her mind screaming to leave the basement!

Before she knew what happened she was standing at the stairs leading to the second floor. She paused, scolding herself.

"What the hell are you doing? Get a grip," she told herself. Taking in several icy gulps of air she calmed her heart and got back in control of her body.

"Everything is fine. The girl in there is dead and can't hurt you." She'd shut the door and texted Dorian. In the morning she'd have Draven help her estimate the water damage and send him into the freezer to fix the light.

Once a plan was created, Thana felt better. The last thing on her list was to warm up. She went up the stairs and back into her bedroom. Her sisters were huddled together in her bed, looking warmer than they had before.

Thana put her keys away and slipped off her shoes, keeping her body language nonchalant.

"Did you find out what's going on?" Morana asked

"No," Thana lied, shrugging. No sense in scaring them. They'd want to know how the freezer door got open and Thana didn't have an answer for them.

"It's really odd," Lola commented.

"Yeah, but I'm sure Dorian can figure it out. He's our handy Mr. Fix It Man." Which was true. Dorian was a life saver. If he couldn't fix it he'd know someone who could, and at a discount.

Thana shut her bedroom door and climbed in after her sisters. The electric blanket and the mountain of other comforters and quilts they'd piled on the bed did the trick. She started to warm up, pinpricks of pain sliding over her cold skin as it heated.

"We should bury her tomorrow," Morana said into the silence.

"We already talked about this. I think that's a good plan. She has a grave already, she should go into it," Thana said.

"She can't in the state it was in. We don't want people coming to gawk at her or dig her up," Lola said, yawning. She snuggled down until only the top of her head and eyes were visible.

"She has a point," Thana acknowledged.

"How soon do you think Dorian could put up a stone wall and padlocked gate?" Morana asked.

"As soon as we can clear out all that grass and put her in there," Thana said.

"Morana and I will do the grass and weeds tomorrow. You get some…what…gravediggers, here asap and then we'll put a pretty and efficient wall around her," Lola said.

"We will?" Morana asked, on her side, facing Lola.

"Yes, that way Thana isn't doing all the work."

"Go to sleep," Thana said, rolling her eyes.

Soon she could hear Lola's tiny snores and the deep breathing that meant both her sisters had fallen asleep. But Thana couldn't sleep. Her eyes stared at the closed door and her mind wandered to the basement.

Anxiety filled up her bosom until sleep was impossible, but she loathed the idea of getting out of her warm bed to wander the inhospitable house. Sticking a hand out from under the blankets she could tell the air was warming up, but not by much.

The clock on the wall read 4 a.m. and Thana knew she wouldn't sleep again. She thought about Draven and all the mysteries that surrounded him. He knew more than what he was telling her, she was sure of it. It hadn't stopped her from wishing he'd been with her while she was frightened.

Grabbing her phone, she sent off a text, knowing it was a long shot he'd be up.

She was wrong. Within seconds her phone vibrated against her leg.

I was just thinking about you. Why are you up so early?

Why are you? She texted back.

Always am, I don't sleep a lot.

It was cold and I couldn't get back to sleep. The truth was way more than texting could handle.

It may be expected and corny, but I could warm you up.

More than corny, an awful pickup line. She giggled. Morana made a noise and Thana quieted down.

But true, you've been avoiding me since I took you in the cemetery.

I don't know if we should do that again. And she didn't; she wanted to, but she didn't need a fuck boy in her life and wasn't sure what Draven wanted. She didn't think he was the relationship type.

We should and we should do it often.

You are like fire and ice...confusing.

I know, and I'm sorry. But after our first kiss, I have thought about touching you again, often. It didn't stop just because you moved away. As I've proved more than once.

You could have contacted me again.

Lorelei made me promise not to. She wanted you to have a life away from Hill City. I respected that. That one time, it had to be just that, nothing more.

Thana paused, fingers on the screen; she didn't know what to say next. Minutes passed.

Thana?

Sorry, I was thinking.

I seem to make you do that a lot.

You keep things from me, and I don't like it. Why was it so much easier to talk with him through an electronic device with space between them? That couldn't be a healthy way to start a relationship, or even maintain a friendship.

I would tell you everything if I could.

I had a dream tonight about a story my aunt told me once.

She liked to tell stories. Which one was it?

Remember the one about the widow who slept with death to save a village?

Thana waited, increasingly nervous as time passed with no response. Her legs were starting to sweat under her pants, a good sign the house was warming up.

Yes, just as I remember the last time we spoke about it.

Is it about my family?

Kind of. It's the story of *The Girl Who Cures Death*; Dabria

I thought it might be, though she's taken liberties with it.

You'd be surprised how many she didn't take.

What does that mean? How could it not be exaggerated? No one died freeing a village from a plague and bringing the dead back to life.

I have things to do before I come over. I must go. I look forward to seeing you in the morning.

Thana looked toward the window. Even through the clouds she could see it was lightening to proper day.

It's morning now.

So, it is.

THIRTEEN

"I don't know what to tell you, but there's no trace of ice anywhere or water damage," Dorian said. He was standing in the kitchen after inspecting the entire property.

It was 9:00 a.m. and the house was back to its normal appearance and temperature.

When she'd finally stumbled out of bed at 6:00 a.m. to shower, she couldn't tell anything odd transpired during the night. If her sisters hadn't been affected, she might consider it all a junk food-induced dream.

She showered and changed from her sweats to a black A-line dress with a red belt and knee-high boots. She threw her hair back into the severe bun she always wore when conducting business and went down into the kitchen.

There was no ice anywhere, no puddles of water and no cold spots from the night before. She went into her office and got on the phone, to work then.

Her sisters didn't come downstairs until 8:00 a.m. and Dorian showed up soon after.

"Well, we didn't all have the same hallucination," Morana said. She was making brioche French toast and forcing a third helping on Lola. Their middle sister's face held a bemused expression as she humored Morana.

"I didn't say that, Miss, I saw the pictures. But now everything looks fine. Thank your stars it does because from what you described that could have been an expensive nightmare." Dorian gripped his hat in his hands, looking nervous. He'd done a wonderful job with the renovations, but he still hated coming inside, preferring to hire outsiders instead to do the inner work.

"Thanks for coming over so quickly, Dorian. The rain let up?" Thana asked, glancing out the window.

"Yes, if the good weather holds, I hope to have the exterior done within the week. The crematory is almost finished."

"That reminds me, I need to add a small project on to the to-do list," Thana said.

Dorian smiled, more work equaled more money. "Decided to add the carport as we discussed?"

"No, I still think that would hurt the building's aesthetics. There is a small grave in the forest. Do you know of it?"

Dorian shook his head no, which was surprising. The way most the town people acted, she thought it'd be common knowledge.

"You don't know the story?" Lola asked.

"No, but I don't live in Hill City, remember?" Dorian asked.

She didn't think it a good idea to tell him about the body in the basement. "There's an old fence around it that's pretty beat up. I want to take it down and put up a stone wall and gate with a new lock."

Dorian scratched his chin looking thoughtful, then he nodded. "That should be very doable. Let me think about it and I'll come up with some plans and designs. When do you want it installed?"

"End of the week," Thana said. Both her sisters looked at her, Morana covering shock on her face.

"Okay, well I'm off, work to be done," Dorian said.

"You don't want breakfast? There's plenty," Lola offered, waving to the huge buttered stack of French toast on the counter.

"No, Miss Lola. In fact, most of my crew, myself included, have gained five pounds since we started working for you."

"I'm making enchiladas for lunch!" Morana called out to him. He laughed harder but still left.

"The end of the week?" Lola asked.

"That's in four days!" Morana exclaimed. She wiped her hand on her jeans, her red long-sleeved shirt was already stained with butter and read, "I Kissed a Chef and I Liked It." She was in full makeup, hair fluffed around her face.

They were planning to go into town for a few hours to grocery shop and pick up household essentials before tackling the overgrown grave. She hated drawing attention to herself and *it*.

"While you two were snoring away the morning, I got up and made a few calls. I found a company from Portland who can come Friday and dig the grave. I am having to pay them extra because they won't be able to bring in their normal equipment. With the space, it will have to be dug by hand, which can take several hours."

"Are you going to embalm her first?" Lola asked, her long hair was braided and looked shiny in the morning light. Thana's eyes chased a dust particle before resettling on her sister's face.

Lola looked so much better, the bruises fading, and soon the only scars would be internal. She was in a white sweater dress, a yellow scarf around her neck and white leggings. Beige leather boots completed her outfit.

"No, I think letting her thaw and decompose naturally is a much better way to go."

"People will be furious. Not only will people not talk about Dabria, but several have told us to leave her alone, down in the freezer," Morana cautioned.

"This was your idea, Morana. Would you rather we left her in the freezer?" Thana asked, which was impossible. Inspectors were coming in a week. The body had to go.

"No, she can't stay down there. We just won't tell anyone," Lola said. She got up and went to the sink and started loading the dishwasher. Thana watched her, her movements repetitive and soothing to watch.

"In this town? It won't stay secret for long. Someone is bound to notice. Most likely Draven, or that weird old lady we met in the woods," Morana huffed, leaning against the counter, hands shoved into the pockets of her black trousers.

"I have people coming to inspect downstairs. Do you really think I'll pass inspection and get the permits I need updated and signed off on when they see the girl downstairs? There are laws about how long you can keep a corpse. Especially one without a proper death certificate or any identifying information aside from a family legend," Thana said.

"We could hide her when they come," Morana suggested.

"Why are you being like this?" Thana asked. Morana was stubborn and argumentative, but she'd been on board with this idea less than twenty-four hours before.

"Don't you think it's a bit strange, some of the things that have happened here over the weeks?" she asked. She wouldn't meet Thana's eyes.

The sound of clanking dishes and water gradually came to a halt, the smell of soap filling the room.

"You're kidding, right?" Lola asked, incredulously, staring at Morana like she'd grown another head.

"What are you talking about?" Morana asked. She had that tone in her voice, the backpedaling one.

"Are you actually saying you think the corpse downstairs is causing the issues we've had?" Lola asked, drying her hands on the mint colored tea towel hanging from the stove, dishes forgotten.

"I don't know. Maybe? Maybe we should go to Portland. You can stay with Trixie and me."

"Rats abandoning the ship," Thana said, smirking.

"I am not going anywhere. Don't lump me in with her," Lola said, then she pointed a finger at Morana, "and you! I thought you outgrew such nonsense fears. Lorelei told us those stories to scare us as children. There are no such things as monsters, curses or ghosts. I've met real monsters and believe me I'd take on a ghost any day instead of that."

Her face was red and her breathing shallow. She was shaking with quiet rage.

Thana made to put an arm around her, but Lola put up a hand. Their universal signal for "No, don't come any closer. I'm fine."

"I'm going upstairs. When I come back, be ready to go into town." She stomped off to the upstairs.

"Good going, Morana," Thana teased her younger sister. For a second all she could see was the little girl Morana used to be, bright red birthmark on her cheek, hiding behind her hair.

Anger leaked out of Thana like a balloon with a pinhole. She couldn't blame Morana. She'd had several moments of fear since coming back to Forgotten Hills. She was just smart enough not to voice them out loud.

"I didn't mean to upset her," Morana said, voice stiff with checked emotion.

"I know you didn't. She'll calm down and forgive you. She always does. Lola forgives everyone."

"Sometimes too easily." Morana looked toward the stairs leading to the second floor, a blank expression on her face.

"What are you thinking?" Thana asked, moving closer to her sister, about to offer comfort and Morana lifted her hand, just as Lola had a moment before.

"That I don't envy you having to stay here after we leave. I'll put my shit aside for Lola, but…"

"But if things get creepier, you're bailing?" Thana asked, heat in her words. No matter her tough exterior, Morana would always be the timid and frightened thing she was as a child, needing Lola and Thana to protect her. For a moment she'd gotten to play hero, helping save Lola, but Thana knew she really wanted to go back to Trixie and her bakery.

"Yeah, and I'll want Lola to come with me," Morana said.

"Whatever, Morana. I'll do it by myself, like always." She was in the hall before she heard Morana's whispered, "Not fair."

Thana slammed through the door, furious in a way that only a sister can make you.

She missed that Draven was at his desk. She stalked past him, mind on so many other things. She didn't hear him call her name, then call it again.

When a hand grasped her elbow she turned, violently.

"Hey, hey!" he said a worried look in those odd eyes.

"Oh…sorry…" She blew a breath out and then drew it back in, slowly. "Sorry, I was…preoccupied."

"You guys get in a fight?"

"Kind of…how could you tell?" She tried to laugh it off.

"As close as you are, I remember a lot of afternoons where you'd storm through the ring. That same angry, pained and exasperated look on your face. Yes, the one you're wearing now. You'd tell me about some tiff you guys had and then it'd be over. I'd hear you hours later laughing together."

"Wait, you used to listen to us?" she asked. She let him

draw her to a chair and they sat down. He took her hand in his, running his thumb over the palm.

"Sometimes it was the babbling of three streams colliding. I envied it. It's not like that with my…siblings."

"You have siblings?"

Running a hand through his hair his face holding stress he said, "Yeah, we don't always…get on well."

"How many?" She didn't want to pry but she wanted to know, badly. He never spoke about his family or his life.

"Three and we are very different."

"If you want, we could invite them to the re-opening party."

His eyes closed and he took a deep breath, "I appreciate the thought, but no."

Thana bit her lip, pondering his words. She couldn't imagine not being close to her sisters.

"The only thing we have in common is darkness," Draven said.

"I'm sure there's more." Thana placed a hand on his knee, threading his fingers through hers as he took a deep breath.

"When we were younger, of course. Now, what's on the agenda for today?"

She told him all about the ice and cold and how shaken her sisters were. She didn't want to tell him she was planning to bury Dabria, it would only upset him.

"Not good. What do you think was the cause?" Draven asked when she paused to take a breath.

"I don't know, but it didn't feel normal. Lola wants Dabria out of the basement and Morana is considering going back to Portland because the place might be haunted."

"I warned you not to mess with her," Draven said, his voice and face giving nothing away.

"You can't really believe she's responsible. There's no such thing as ghosts."

"Have you ever been out in the cemetery at night?" Draven changed the subject.

"No."

"Why not?" he asked it like he already knew the answer.

"We never go out there after dark. Aunt Lorelei said it isn't safe." Was this a test?

"Did she say why not?"

"No, we always assumed she worried about us hurting ourselves or wild animals."

"The cemetery has many secrets, Thana. Your aunt believed at night those secrets became corporeal and wandered the ground."

"That's crazy, but I'm not surprised. Lorelei was eccentric." *Yes, eccentric, but not crazy*—a little voice in the back of her mind said. If Lorelei was afraid of something there was a possibility it was real.

"Just be careful." He was leaning in. He was going to kiss her. Thana's eyes fluttered closed.

No kiss came. Instead a rush of air and her eyes opened to find Draven moving back to his desk as the door to the hallway opened and her sisters came through. Their smiles meant they'd made up.

"You ready to go?" Lola asked, not acknowledging Draven at all.

"I'm driving!" Morana called out.

"Alright, but only if we take my car." Reaching in the pocket of her skirt she pulled out her crowded key chain and threw it at Morana. Her sister caught it and grimaced. "You could kill a man with these."

"Only ten percent why I keep it."

They all laughed, Thana's cutting off short. In the corner of her eye, she swore there was someone in the window near her. A woman looking in, eyes pure black.

FOURTEEN

HILL CITY WAS A TINY TOWN. THERE WASN'T A STOP LIGHT and the main road consisted of several little shops that catered to the small number of tourists they got every year. The theatre, a grocery store, diner, two bed and breakfasts, a small hospital, a nursing home and a gas station made up the rest. From the main road several others veined off, taking you to the police station, several churches, residential areas, two schools, and other utility buildings. There were about 3,500 people that lived in Hill City. Most over the age of fifty.

Morana pulled into an empty spot outside the grocery store. It was a bright, clean and shining building with large glass windows with signs declaring sales on ground beef, disinfecting wipes, and creamed corn.

"Wow, Shirley's sure hasn't changed," Lola said. They stood around looking at the neon blue light stating, *Welcome to Shirley's!* and underneath a small sign read: *Best Produce For twenty miles!*

"Most of Hill City hasn't, except maybe a little sprucing, the colors look brighter than I remember," Thana said. She was distracted with thoughts of the woman she'd seen in the glass, had it been real? Was she going crazy? And could she convince herself it was simply a warped reflection?

"Well, are you coming?" Morana asked. She already had a cart. Lola stood next to her, list in hand.

Thana nodded and then stopped dead in her tracks. She'd seen something, something she never thought she'd see again. A little bright green Volvo parked in front of Hill Bed and Breakfast.

"No, no, you guys should be fine. I'm going to wander," she told them. Her sisters shrugged.

"Suit yourself, give us twenty, tops," Lola said.

Thana crossed the street. It didn't even have painted divider lines. She walked up to the car.

"It can't be," she said, hugging herself—suddenly cold.

A glance in the driver's side confirmed her suspicion. A bobbly head alien, green and chipping was stuck to the dashboard.

Thana spun, quickly, she had to get out of there. Heart racing in her chest, it felt like she couldn't get enough air.

"Thana!"

She didn't want to stop, but if she'd already been seen, what was there to do? Hide? She was a grown woman after all.

So instead she stopped, and took several deep breaths.

"Thana! Could you at least turn around and look at me? I came all this way to see you," the thick Hispanic voice was only feet behind her.

"Could we also not do this in the street? Please?"

Thana faced the voice. "Dani, what are you doing here?"

Dani was petite, with dark skin and the largest brown eyes. When they first met those eyes had drawn Thana in.

Dani had short curly brown hair cropped close to the skull and liked to wear vintage clothes. If they were pinstriped or argyle the better.

"I wanted to see you," Dani said, her mouth turned up at the corners, those pouty lips that Thana once adored and then learned to hate.

"I don't want to see you," Thana said, gritting her teeth.

"Can we not do this in the street? I don't want to be small-town drama. The place I'm staying has a little patio. Please give me ten minutes?" Dani begged.

"Fine," Thana said following her ex-girlfriend.

They went to the side of Hill B & B, through a little white gate and into a small patio filled with roses and hummingbird feeders. Cobblestones and colored glass made up the path to a set of white wire chairs with pale blue padding.

"I can't believe you never brought me here! Hill City is a treasure!" Dani said, sitting down.

"Dani, we broke up months ago. What the hell are you doing here?"

"I wanted to talk to you to see if we could fix things."

Thana sat down and put her head in her hands. "There isn't anything to fix. You knew what the Lottes were up to. She told me they paid you to keep your mouth shut. The fact that you're not in jail is a miracle."

"Why do you have to be so black and white? I said I was sorry, that I made a mistake. But it paid well. I looked the other way on a few of my bodies and they gave me extra cash. Which I needed to send home to my family…I told you this. Why won't you let it go?"

"It was wrong, and you knew it. If you needed money so badly there are a dozen other options, including getting hired on at a larger company. I don't want to rehash this, Dani. We broke up and I can't believe you followed me here. How long have you been here?"

"A few days, getting up the courage to come see you. I drove by that old cemetery. Even for me, that place looks spooky. I can't let you go, Thana. I love you. I know you loved me. I had to give it one more try." She leaned forward and touched Thana's leg.

Thana didn't flinch, but she didn't lean in either. She didn't feel anything.

"Maybe, we could start again? I could help you out with that mortuary you're restoring," Dani suggested.

"No," Thana said, "I don't love you. I don't know if I ever did."

Dani looked like Thana hit her.

"I don't believe that. Now you're just being cruel. How many times do I have to say I'm sorry and that I was wrong?"

Thana's phone went off. Morana asking where she was. She didn't want her sisters to see this but had a feeling Dani was going to drag it out. Dani always had a talent for making Thana do things she didn't want to.

"I know, I know, you want me to leave, but I can't. Not until I at least get a tour of Forgotten Hills. You used to bore me to tears telling the same stories over and over again. I half thought it was a fairy tale, not real, ya know?" Dani joked.

"A tour?" Thana asked. Ok fine, she could do a tour. If that got Dani, and the painful memories she'd brought with her, to leave.

She texted Morana to leave and that she'd explain when she got back. This got her a *????? Ok, but details asap!!* Text back.

"That one of your sisters?"

"Yeah, they were shopping. I told them I'd get a ride home."

Dani's smile lit up the patio. "See, I knew you'd come around!"

"No, you came out here, you wanted to see me and Forgotten Hills. You'll get your wish and then I want you to leave and not come back, got it?" Thana stood, glaring down at the smaller woman.

Tears filled Dani's eyes. "Yeah, sure, why are you always such a cold bitch, Thana?"

They walked out to Dani's car and Thana got in. It smelled like strawberries. How many times had she ridden in the passenger seat, laughing at Dani as they went to antique stores or old cemeteries? They'd dated for a year before all the trouble with the Lottes. Most memories were good ones. It was too bad they were now tainted and made her queasy to think about.

Dani started the car and they sat in silence. The radio was broken and had been for a decade. Dani sang to pass time, old songs, in Spanish. She told stories about her trips home to see her parents in Mexico, or childhood tales full of misadventure. Dani loved to talk. Thana used to love to listen to her. Thana closed her eyes against the pain and Draven's face swam in her mind. The pain eased and a warmth filled her.

"We were good together, babe. We could be again," Dani finally said, putting the car in reverse. Thana didn't comment or give directions. Dani already admitted she knew where she was going.

Thana had been so sure Dani wasn't involved with the trouble at the Lottes, 100% positive Dani was like herself; innocent of even knowing what was going on. Until Loretta Lotte, a sneer on her face, explained that Dani had known everything. That the bracelet she'd given Thana for Christmas had come off a corpse.

"Wow," Dani said, a few minutes later. They pulled up in front of Forgotten Hills. "This place has to be haunted."

"I don't believe in ghosts, you know that." It felt like a lie.

"You only believe in those sisters of yours, right?" Dani said, bitterness in every word.

Thana gave her a hard look and got out. "Come on, you wanted a tour before leaving. Let's do it."

"You really should paint this place a cheery color. People like cheer," Dani said.

They went up the stairs. Thankfully her sisters weren't in the main room, but Draven was. He rose when he saw her, eyes narrowing.

"Draven, this is Dani. Dani, Draven helps keep Forgotten Hills running," she introduced them.

"Are you alright?" Draven asked, coming around the desk. He put a hand on her shoulder. She let out a breath she didn't know she'd been holding.

"Yeah, just giving an," she paused trying to think of what to say, "an old friend a tour. Then she's leaving."

Thana led Dani into the back. Best place to start a tour? The chapel.

"You need more lights," Dani suggested as they walked the dim hallway into the back. Thana opened one of two large oak doors and flipped a switch lighting up the room. They walked in, leaving the door open.

The chapel was a big room with a small stage at the front. In the back was a side room with a one-way mirror where the funeral director could watch, deal with music and lightning, if necessary and not be in the way. The chapel had eggshell colored walls and forest green carpet. Her aunt had painted vines and flowers on one wall and the lights were a dim yellow. Wooden chairs were stacked in a corner. Toward the front was a curtained off privacy section for family to grieve, without being watched.

The room smelled stale and looked outdated, but Thana had grand plans to repaint and make it bright and fresh.

"No windows?" Dani asked.

"No, my aunt thought it affected privacy."

The only sound in the room was their breathing. Their footprints making indents in the lush carpet.

"It's small."

"There's also a viewing room next door."

"You could only hold one funeral at a time."

"I don't think people here die in droves. This place isn't meant to be like large mortuaries," Thana explained.

"So, is the guy why you don't want me back?" Dani asked.

"Draven? No, we've already talked about this," Thana said, internally groaning. Not this again. Dani was like a dog with a bone.

"I know you, Thana. You don't just let anyone touch you. You decide you wanted to ride a dick again? You bi girls are all the same."

"Don't be nasty, Dani, it doesn't suit you." Thana crossed her arms over her chest. Leave it to Dani to pull the bisexual girls are fickle card rather than admit to herself any kind of truth.

"Are you feeling alright?" Thana asked after a minute or two of silence. Dani looked pale and sickly.

"It's cold in here. Aren't you cold?" Dani took a few steps toward the privacy curtain and froze.

"What's up?"

"Do you see that?" Her voice was barely a whisper.

"See what?" Thana squinted in the curtain's direction. Dani pointed a black tipped nail and Thana's breath caught in her throat.

There was someone or something standing on the other side. The outline was dark, and it didn't move. The curtain wasn't sheer, but it wasn't solid either. She should be able to tell who was standing there.

"Morana? Lola? Is that one of you? What are you doing in here?" Thana called out to the shape. Maybe one of her sisters needed extra privacy. She tried to remember if her car was parked out front. Were her sisters even home yet?

"Hush, don't get its attention!" Dani slapped at her.

"If you've broken in here, I am calling the cops," Thana tried again and pulled out her phone.

Still, whatever it was didn't move.

"I told you this place is haunted," Dani said. She sounded close to crying as she moved behind Thana, gripping her clothes.

Thana ignored her, fear pooling in her belly. What if it was a crazy squatter and they'd been living with it all this time? She recalled the noises she'd heard, the thumping and a lump caught in her throat.

She saw an old flower stand next to the door leading back to the hall. Grabbing it she advanced toward the shadow.

"Thana, no!"

Thana made the decision quickly. She parted the curtain and slashed with the stand, only for the thin metal to meet... air. There was nothing there. Not a person or a piece of furniture.

"It's empty!" she called back, puzzled. Something had to be giving off the dark human-like shadow, right? That's how the world worked. This section smelled like rotting flowers. She'd need to air it out.

Giving the space another visual once-over, she made her way back to Dani.

Dani stood, hands clasped over her mouth, trembling with, what Thana assumed was fright.

Thana looked around the room, trying to figure out what the woman was terrified of. Every ounce of blood left her face when she found it. Something was in the funeral director's booth and she could see it through the mirror, which was impossible.

The same imposing black human-like shape. A shadow on the other side of the mirror.

"What the fuck?" Thana asked. A feeling like ants crawling over her skin overcame her.

"It can see us," Dani squeaked out.

"We should go," Thana decided, motioning to the still open door.

"Yes," Dani said, and they slowly started to move toward the door.

Thana shouldn't have looked back. She should have just gotten the hell out, but she couldn't resist one more look at the thing.

Whatever it was had turned around and now two red eyes glowed from the darkness and it watched her. Then a harsh whisper filled the room, *"Run!"*

Which they did.

They skidded, breathless into the waiting room.

"What was that!" Dani exclaimed.

"I have no idea," Thana said.

"A fucking ghost, and not a nice one." Dani gulped in her air.

"Ghost's aren't real." Again, probably a lie.

"We just saw one! Fuck you, Thana, I take it back. I have no interest in staying here with you. You should have this place blessed or something." Dani righted herself and started toward the door.

She looked back, briefly, eyes darting to the darkened hallway.

"Be safe, ok? I guess this really is goodbye."

"It was goodbye the first time," Thana said. Dani glared and slammed the front door.

"Draven, let's check the entire house and make sure we're the only ones in here," Thana said as she heard Dani start her car. Her fear was lessening and now she felt foolish and angry.

"Except for the ghost."

Thana snorted, "Yeah, except for the ghost."

FIFTEEN

"Do you remember the one-time Mom and Dad came and picked us up early?" Morana asked.

They were in the cemetery, lying on the thick grass near Elder. Lola was making a flower crown and Morana was scribbling in a notebook. She and Trixie were planning to publish their first cookbook.

Thana, her hands under her head, was half asleep, dozing as she counted how many clouds looked like cats.

They were taking the evening off after spending the entire day hard at work. Both her sisters smelled of dirt and grass while Thana spent all day with Draven going through the finances, tax documents and dealing with supplies and ordering. All three girls were exhausted.

She hadn't told them about seeing the girl in the window and the shadow in the chapel. For one, it might scare them or worry them. Secondly, she wasn't sure of what she saw and telling her sisters would make it real. She also didn't want to talk about Dani's visit.

"Earth to Thana," Lola said, throwing a flower, but let's be honest it was really a weed, at her head.

"Oh, what?" Her response caused her sisters to giggle.

"I wonder where your mind went?" Lola asked.

"Probably stuck on an interesting male specimen that works for us," Morana teased.

Lola' face darkened, and her eyes narrowed. "What is that supposed to mean?"

"Oh, Lola, it's obvious she and Draven like each other."

"Hmmm, is that true, Thana?"

"I don't know, maybe?" She did not want to have this conversation right now.

"You've only known him a few weeks," Lola pointed out. "And it's only been six months since you and Dani broke up."

Thana did not want to discuss this. "What did you ask me, Morana?"

"You're changing the subject, but as your face is now a delightful shade of pink, I'll let it slide." Lola went back to her flower crown, one eye still on her sisters.

"I asked do you remember the one-time Mom and Dad picked us up from here early? I was trying to remember. I mean I know they did, and I always have this feeling it went badly."

"Not surprised, you were only four, it wasn't great. I only remember that they fought," Lola said.

"Yeah, they did fight and yes, I remember it."

The end of summer at Forgotten Hills was hot and a little humid. Only the mortuary side of the house and the prep rooms had air conditioning. The rest relied on fans and window AC units, which weren't a lot of help on days hotter than eighty degrees. Normally, Hill City never got much past eighty degrees, but there was always one sweltering hot week in August.

These days found the girls outside in the shade in the early mornings and for an hour or two before the sunset. During those times they did what they always did; chatter, drink mint lemonade and play.

After 9 a.m. little girls could be found in many places.

Morana often curled up next to the freezer eating ice cream she or Lorelei made the day before, usually with a Walkman attached to her ears. When she was four, she played a mix tape Lorelei made her, over and over and wished it wasn't too hot to dance. She'd let the ice cream, normally vanilla with sprinkles, drip down her chin and stain the baggy cream-colored slip she'd stolen from their aunt. She loved how the silk was cool and it was so large on her it pooled over her feet like water. A blanket of slithering cool fabric. Aside from the music, nothing changed as she got older.

Lola would jump in the shower, blasting cold water over her tan skin, washing away dust from the morning. Once done, she wrapped a fuzzy brown towel around her and lay on her stomach under the window ac in the living room. She'd drip dry, shivering as the cold air blew across her skin, causing her hair to frizz. As she waited to dry off, she'd sleep, or work on her cross stitch. She filled sketchbook after sketchbook with drawings. Mythological animals, handsome men with no clear features, elaborate landscapes in black and white and charcoal smudged fingerprints on the page corners.

The prep room was always cold, but Thana hated to disturb her aunt and the idea of hanging out in a sterile environment where her aunt cut open dead bodies wasn't appealing. So, she'd take a pillow and whatever book she was reading and camp out on the top stairs, head on the pillow, feet up against the wall, wearing nothing but her swimsuit. She enjoyed the cold air that wafted up the stairs and the odd music that often accompanied it. Sometimes Lorelei would take a break and sit on the bottom step, talking to her.

During this heat-soaked week, there would always be one day that was different. Where their aunt would get fed up with the heat and take them out. Sometimes swimming until the sand was in every nook and cranny and their skin tanned dark. Other times it was to the small, but air-conditioned, theatre on Main Street. Hill House only played old movies, where you could sit on one of a dozen dilapidated couches or recliners and watch movies like Willie Wonka, A Muppet Movie, and Wizard of Oz. Sometimes these trips included a visit to the soda fountain in the pharmacy where a pimple-faced boy served them chocolate sodas. Other times a stop at the pizza parlor for dinner, as it was "too god damn hot" to turn the stove on.

Occasionally she'd pack them in her truck and take them to Pineville, driving fast with the windows down. Pineville had a mall, though that was being kind. It was really a large building with half a dozen shops attached to a Woolworths. They'd wander around the small building, where most stores were out of business or doing so poorly the people watched them, hungry for their business. They'd eat big soft pretzels, licking salt from fingertips and often Lorelei would buy them new books from Walden Books store.

The one place you'd never find them on the hot days was in the mortuary proper. Lorelei told them they were more than welcome to watch TV in her office and relish the cool air conditioning. They never did. Crossing the threshold from the hallway to the receptionist area was too much like trying to edge into a forbidden land. When they were small it was a game. Who could get closest to the front door before being a chicken and running back.

The mortuary side of Forgotten Hills was a different place. Lola hated it because sometimes you could hear the families crying through the walls. Morana detested it because she knew at any time there could be dead bodies sleeping in their caskets of wood and satin lining. She imagined them climbing out at night to whisper about the living. Thana just didn't like the idea of three dirty wild girls running about a business where people came to mourn their dead. It wasn't respectful to be watching Days of Our Lives in a cool room while some mother grieved for her baby down the hall.

Only once did the girls ever willingly go into the mortuary. They went and hunkered down under the window near the front door and listened. They listened to the two women outside argue.

The summer Thana was eleven, her parents came to get them early. They moved during the summer. Not unusual, just unwelcome, and associated with where their parents took the next job. Whether her mother found a better teaching position, or her father decided to switch hospitals.

In the nineteen years Thana lived with her parents they moved eight times and six of those times they did it with no warning. Nothing like arriving at an airport in an unknown city having no idea where your new home was, what your room looked like or if your parents remembered to pack all of your stuff.

They lived in Phoenix, Tuscon, Tempe, and Flagstaff Arizona all by the time Thana was eight. They moved to Nashville when she was fourteen and Cambridge the year she turned seventeen. But this particular time was when her parents moved them to Houston.

They gave Lorelei no warning, just showed up.

"You could have called, sent a letter or anything. I've still got two weeks with them," Lorelei said. They could hear the anger in her voice. It was new. Their aunt never yelled and never became cross.

"We got the call last minute. I'm only glad we checked our messages, or we'd have missed it. Two slots at their new school are hard to hold onto, everyone wants in," their mother's chilly voice.

"Why does she always sound like that? It's like she doesn't

understand how her decisions could affect others," Thana huffed, arms crossed over her small frame as she leaned against the wall.

Lola shushed her.

"Maria, come on. Why don't you and Peter stay the night at least. We can have dinner together and then you can leave in the morning. It would be nice to share a meal together as a family."

"No. I won't step foot in that place, and you know it. Now I'd appreciate it if you got the girls packed and brought them out to me."

"I'm not your fucking servant, Maria. If you want them to go with you so badly you can come inside and help them pack. They are your children, after all." This was a side of their aunt they never saw. Bitter...mean.

"Don't be like that, Lorelei. You love having the girls here and are upset I'm taking them away earlier than normal. Now please, we have a hotel room in Portland and an early flight in the morning."

"Wait...if you're staying the night why waste money at a hotel, especially when there's room here! The girls will be really upset if you simply yank them away from all their fun," now their aunt was pleading.

A laugh came from their mother. "Their fun? More like their studies."

"Studies?" Thana asked at the same time Lorelei did.

"Yes, don't think I don't hear them repeating your stories. You're training them to take over when you die."

"I don't have a choice. I can't train my own child. I don't have any to train if you'll remember." There was something in Lorelei's voice Thana didn't understand, a hidden message inside the grief.

"You made your own choices years ago and I made mine. You get them the entire summer, until a week before school.

Which is right now. When I left here, I swore I wouldn't come back and I've already stood on the porch longer than I'd care to. No way are Peter and I coming inside, let alone sleeping here."

"Please don't take them yet." Thana almost missed her aunt's whisper.

There was silence for several long seconds.

"You agreed to this. I am sorry, Lorelei, but we have to go. Their education is more important than another two weeks."

Wide-eyed, Thana held her hand up and jerked it toward the door. The three of them scurrying to get back to the kitchen before Lorelei came in and stumbled upon them eavesdropping.

"I wonder why mom hates it here?" Lola asked. She'd finished the flower crown and settled it atop her head.

"Probably because we are the Keepers of the Dead," Thana repeated what Draven told her and about the graves.

"Wow, yeah I'd want to leave too. I love it here, but it sounds like Lorelei was trapped under family obligation," Morana said.

"I think she loved it here as we do, and she had an affinity for the dead like Thana. Mom didn't need to worry. She was never going to be Keeper of the Dead, or whatever," Lola said.

"What if none of us wanted to be in charge of Forgotten Hills, what then?" Thana asked. It was a question that lingered at the back of her mind. What if one day she changed her mind?

"What if is a stupid question. We need to focus on the here and now," Morana told her, glaring. "There are things to deal with right now, not in an alternate reality where you don't want to be a mortician."

"What kind of things? Aren't we on top of everything? Dead girl is going in the ground and Forgotten Hills is reviving. Everything is going according to plan. Have you seen the new, what is it, crematorium? It looks great!" Lola exclaimed.

It did. The polished stone walls were clean, steady and made it look like a small addition rather than a place the dead burned. Inside was sterile with white walls awash with light.

"I was talking about you," Morana sighed.

"Oh, well, I'm content to stay as I am for the moment."

"You are welcome to stay here as long as you like. I'll find work for you to do. This place is all of ours," Thana said. She raised up on her arms to look at Lola's face.

"It's yours more. Aunt Lorelei knew you'd be perfect for this place," Lola said.

"It will be lonely when you both leave." Thana rolled into a sitting position.

"Not going anywhere any time soon," Lola said in a sing-song tone.

"We'll come visit all the time." Morana reached out and took Thana's hand.

"Sure, 'cause Trixie will want to vacation in a tiny town and stay in a mortuary." Thana laughed at the image of petite and prim Trixie romping through the cemetery.

"Well, we may have to free up some of our inheritance. Maybe put a guest house behind the crematorium, though seeing the trees chopped down would be sad."

"A guest house? For what? You and Trixie would be plenty comfortable in your room, it has a queen size bed in it," Lola said. She'd started on a new crown, holding stems up to Morana's head for sizing.

Morana blushed. "We didn't want to say anything until

everything was good, you know? Then…then…Lola got hurt and I felt it would be in bad taste."

"What are you talking about?" Lola asked.

"They tell you to wait twelve weeks, but there were complications, so we waited until…"

"You're pregnant!" Thana squealed, launching at Morana to grip her in a hug.

"No, Trixie is." Morana was grinning from ear to ear.

"How far along?" Lola asked in a quiet voice.

Morana and Thana looked at their sister, in time to see her powder blue eyes fill with tears that she viciously dashed away.

"Six and a half months. I'm sorry, Lola. I don't want you to be sad. We were going to tell you at sixteen weeks when we got the last test result. Then you got…hurt and there just didn't seem to be a good time," Morana said, sheepishly.

"I'm happy for you, really I am. I wish you had told us sooner and it makes me mad at myself you hid this special news because you were sparing my feelings." Lola got on her knees and scrambled over to them so the three could embrace.

"Why is Trixie the one who's pregnant? What kind of sperm did you use?" Thana asked. They sat in a tight circle, holding hands.

"We looked through donors and ordered off an online bank. Donor number 33567 was the winner. Ph.D. in Molecular Biology, does BBQ contests, Cuban heritage and didn't have any weird medical issues in his background."

"And…" Thana raised an eyebrow as her sister was evading the question.

"And…no way was I bringing a child into this world with a possibility of *it*. I am even more sure of my choice now that I know mom and Lorelei had *it* too."

"I expect the kid to be named after me," Thana said, changing the subject.

"What if it's a boy?" Morana said, laughing

"Thano, of course."

"Please, Dolores is a much better name."

"Again, what if it's a boy?"

"Still Dolores." This earned a playful punch from Morana.

Lola tipped over, laughing. The sound filled the area like bells tinkling then the laughter stopped abruptly. "Hey, did you know this statue has a hidden compartment?"

Lola had fallen near the base of a weeping angel statue, her face on the grass inches from the base.

"Of course. All of them have one. I used to store treasures in there when I was younger. Why, is there something in there?" Thana crawled over to her sister and saw a faint outline at the bottom. It was cracked open a centimeter.

"Cool, open it!" Morana exclaimed from behind them, peering over Thana's shoulder.

"Spiders," Lola warned.

"Fine." Thana moved away and came back with a large stick.

Thana wedged the stick into the small opening and giving a firm push she moved the panel, a thin slab of marble, slowly back. The noise it made was akin to fingernails on the chalkboard. Each of them flinched.

Morana got out her phone and turned the flashlight on, sending a beam of light into the dark hole under the angel.

"Probably space for an urn," Thana said. A musty smell like a room shut up for too long came wafting out. Lola sneezed.

"I don't think it's empty..." Morana held the light closer. The area wasn't very big. At the back was a package.

"Okay, who wants to reach in, get it and possibly have a creepy crawly come with it? Like that scene in Temple of Doom," Lola said.

"Spiders do not hide out in spaces like this. How would it

eat?" Thana asked though she wasn't sure that information was completely accurate. Gripping the stick again, the rough bark digging into her skin, she used it to snag the package and bring it closer to the opening so she could get it easier.

Thana held a parcel wrapped in several grocery bags, presumably to protect it from the elements. Her sisters gathered around her, each eager to see what it was.

"If you're about to open an envelope with body parts in it, I'm out," Morana warned.

Thana didn't answer her. Once she'd breached the layers of plastic there was a large red leather Filofax. In the left corner was an embroidered name in gold: Lorelei Muerticillo. In the center written in large print was her handwriting. It said, *For Thana.*

SIXTEEN

"Okay, so let's open it," Lola said. They were sitting around the kitchen table.

"Are you sure that's a good idea. She hid it for a reason," Morana said.

"It has my name on it. She obviously wanted me to have it," Thana said.

"But why hide it there and not say anything?" Morana asked.

"I think she knew I'd find it. I used to stash things there during the summer." Thana held the Filofax. It was heavy and filled to bursting.

"Like a band-aid, Thana," Lola said, nudging her with a bare toe.

Thana opened it and took out three pieces of paper from the top. They were folded, thick and cream colored. She opened the first one, running a finger over the raised seal, taking in the fancy print. A glance at the top of each page provided her with each of their names.

Thana Avye Muerticillo

Date of Birth November 1st, 1983

Dolores Samara Muerticillo

Date of Birth: April 30th, 1986

Morana Vedette Muerticillo

Date of Birth: September 1st, 1991

"I think these are our birth certificates."

"Just like Mom to have Lorelei keep them. Wonder why they weren't with the rest of her papers?" Morana snatched hers, rubbing a thumb over the document.

"This doesn't look like the one I have at home," Lola said, frowning.

She was right. They each had a copy of their birth certificate, of course, you need it for...well...everything. She'd never paid much attention to it, but she would have noticed this deviation.

Thana couldn't speak for a second as she finished reading her birth certificate, "I think..." she swallowed, hard, "I think it's because of what they say."

"Wait." Lola was reading hers. "This must be a mistake."

"What.the.fuck," Morana growled. They both looked to their big sister.

As plain as day, the birth certificate listed their parents: Peter Andrews and Lorelei Muerticillo.

"This isn't possible," Thana whispered.

"What does this mean? Were dad and Aunt Lorelei fucking?" Morana asked.

"I don't remember her being pregnant, do you?" Lola asked.

Thana thought about it. She'd have been too young to remember Lorelei pregnant with Lola but...

One summer it rained every day. Lola and Thana were stuck in the house for what seemed like weeks and Lorelei was busy. It was unusual for her to be too busy to play with them. When she wasn't downstairs plying her trade, she was asleep upstairs or busy in her office. Thana remembered she was always on the phone.

She'd made them rose and honey candy one afternoon and tried to explain she was sick and couldn't take them on the grand adventures they were used to. At eight, Thana didn't understand. She just wanted to play, not spend her whole summer looking out for Lola who was five.

Thana never talked back to Lorelei and Lola never cried at her house or threw fits. The first time Thana ever saw Lorelei upset at them was when they both had tiny temper tantrums with small hands balled into fists, tears of anger stinging their eyes.

The cause of their outrage was their aunt leaving them in the care of a teenage babysitter so she could go into Portland without them, for the third time. It was bad enough they only had a week of their vacation left, but why was their aunt leaving?

Lorelei sent them to their rooms where they hugged their knees and cried into blankets until their eyes were red and puffy.

Thinking back and looking over the events of that summer she saw things in her memories she hadn't before. The tall thin man with the briefcase who visited Lorelei several times. How their aunt felt rounder and firmer than normal when she hugged them. Some mornings it took her longer to leave the bathroom, and no matter what candle Lorelei lit, there was always a tinge of sour in the air if you went in after her. Their aunt's odd obsession with chicken tacos and mango jelly. Thana remembered Lorelei canned it herself, the counters covered in the jewel-toned orange concoction.

Also, their mother called every day and not to talk to Lola or Thana.

"I think I do, but she tried really hard to make sure we didn't," Thana said.

"Oh!" Lola's eyes lit up. "The summer we got grounded for two days for talking back."

Thana nodded slowly.

"Lorelei grounded you? No way. She never punished us. I can't even remember her raising her voice, not once." Morana crossed her arms over her chest.

Picking up a sealed envelope she opened it and found court documents in blocky typewritten letters.

Scanning it she tried to sum up what she read. "This is adoption paperwork. They used Lorelei as a surrogate."

"That doesn't make sense. If they were simply using her as a walking incubator she wouldn't be listed under mother."

"It was traditional surrogacy, Morana. It means Lorelei's eggs and dads sperm. We aren't mom's biological children."

"Lorelei was our mom?" Lola gasped.

"Biologically yes, but we were legally Mom and Dad's. Lorelei gave up all her parental rights." Thana put the paperwork on the table, in case her sisters wanted to look at it. Neither made a move to touch it.

"This is too much." Morana stood up, chair scratching against the floor.

"Wait, don't you want to see what else is in here?" Thana called after her as Morana reached the stairs and went up.

"Should we go after her?" Thana asked.

"Not yet, she's probably calling mom." Lola said, "What else is in there?"

Thana went back to the Filofax.

There was an envelope filled with pictures of Lorelei pregnant. Photos of each baby right after birth, names in ink on the back. Pictures of tired, red-eyed Lorelei in a hospital bed holding each of them were also contained within.

Three small slim notebooks bore each of their names.

Blue with "Morana" scrawled across the top, Thana opened it and a lock of hair tied with a ribbon fell out.

Hospital bracelets were taped inside. Dozens of dates and notes from hospital visits.

Thana read a few sentences out loud. "Cravings: chicken tacos (beef makes me puke), homemade mango jelly (store-bought kind is gross). Complications and Annoyances: Ankles swollen to ten times normal size, severe insomnia, no nesting as of yet- I have an incredible urge to bake, but I cannot eat anything I make."

Thana showed the book to Lola so she could see that under Morana's stats from her birth was a description; the size, location, and color of *it*.

"There's also details later of interesting things she did and funny things Morana said during our summers here. Lorelei's hopes and dreams for her and anxiety she wasn't bonding well to Mom." Thana put the book down, Morana would want it.

Lola grabbed a pink book with her name. She quickly flipped through pages that Thana assumed was more of the same.

"May 31st, 1992: Lola came sliding into the kitchen very upset. She wanted to know if we could make the squirrels bathing suits and dresses as she couldn't believe I let them run around Forgotten Hills naked." Lola laughed.

"August 3rd, 1995: Lola cried all afternoon because they are going home tomorrow. She hates her bedroom at home. Says a man watches her from the closet. I will sew some sage yarn into a shawl and add tassels with agates and send it for Christmas."

"I remember that shawl. It looked like sunsets. You wore it every night for over a year," Thana said.

"It's upstairs...in my...baby box," Lola said, voice small. She shut the book and held it close.

Thana's book was black, her name in silver. It was fatter than the others and full of everything one would put in a baby book. A lock of hair, a tooth she lost one summer, medical bracelets, a few photos and an ultrasound picture. She listed dates and information from each doctor's visit. There were also notes on home birth and naturally handling labor pain.

"This says she craved fresh cucumber and corn salsa and even the smell of fish made her puke. She's written down her dreams, states they were vivid. That some were crazy, some were of the past and a few she thought were of future events."

"Lorelei never said she was clairvoyant," Lola commented. Thana only shrugged.

She read out loud, "I dreamed of a woman in her thirties standing in my cemetery, her periwinkle eyes just like mine, ebony curls falling in front of her face. She was speaking to a man. She was talking to death, in love with death. I wanted to pull her away, make her come back to the house. It was so cold, the grass beneath my feet wet and freezing. She couldn't hear me. Then she turned around and I cried out because in her eyes wasn't life. The bright shine of the living had been replaced by the deep sinister sheen of death. She bore our family mark."

"Wow, creepy. I guess the storytelling thing was something she always had," Lola said.

Thana shivered and nodded, "Yeah, I guess so." She shut the book and put it back in the Filofax, unnerved. Had her aunt dreamed about her, all grown up? And if she had, what did it mean? Or maybe it didn't mean anything. Maybe it was simply a pregnancy fueled fever dream.

Thana felt tears threaten in her own eyes. She closed them, squinting hard. She hated to cry, what a waste of time.

She shut the Filofax hard and cradled it to her chest.

"Look," Lola said, pointing down. A slim envelope bearing Thana's name must have slipped from the pages. It lay on the table, mocking her.

"Read it. Maybe it's an explanation." Lola looked hopeful.

Betrayal and deep despair rolled through Thana's chest

and stomach, like a monster thrashing against her ribs. She took a deep breath and picked the envelope up.

Lorelei was their birth mother?

"Do you think this is why mom was distant sometimes?" Thana asked.

Lola considered the question, her cheeks were colorless, her eyes held pain. But she wasn't crying. She was sitting very still.

"No, I don't. To do surrogacy three times means she wanted us. It's not always a pleasant experience. She loved us and did her best. I just think Mom is...well...Mom."

With slow deliberation, Thana opened the envelope. One sheet of paper covered in her aunt's handwriting, front and back.

"Will you read it out loud?" Lola asked, eyes hungry. She was desperate to know what the letter said. Thana knew that because she had the same feeling, as well as fear.

"Should we wait for Morana?" Thana asked. She held the paper too tight and crinkled the edges.

Lola hopped out of her chair and went to the stairs, cocking her head and listening.

"No. I think she's yelling at Mom."

"Okay, here goes."

SEVENTEEN

Querida,

Like any good story, this one should start at the beginning. Once upon a time, yes once upon a time, don't grimace, you'll get wrinkles.

There were two sisters. Both beautiful in their own way. One creative and one smart. We will call them Mary and Sue. They were very close when they were younger, but as they grew up, they grew apart.

Mary, the eldest, held family secrets close to her chest and studied hard to take over the enchanting business they called home. She studied her family history, kept the language and their traditions.

Sue didn't want to stay in a moldy old museum to the dead. She didn't care about her heritage. She wanted to go to college and explore the world. She wanted to marry and have babies. While Mary planned to shut herself away and be the Keeper of the Dead for all eternity, Sue wanted to have adventures and create her life anew.

Their parents died when the girls were twenty-one and eighteen. Sue took her portion of the life insurance money and ran, promising never to come back. For you see, there were things in their home that once seen could not be unseen and there was a burden of being born into their family. A mark- placed on the skin while in the womb so death would recognize you.

Mary built a solid and interesting life by herself, but she missed her sister. Sue only called once a year; on Christmas and would accept no calls or parcels outside of that time frame.

Then Sue broke her promise. She turned up on the front porch heartbroken and in tears. Her womb empty and worried she would lose her new husband if she could not give him children.

Mary did the only thing she could think of. She offered her own healthy body to grow children. Why waste the eggs she had when her sister so desperately wanted to be a mother?

What Mary never counted on was growing attached. Learning to love each hiccup, smiling at tiny feet kicking her from the inside, finding joy at her rounded belly and the life growing inside it. She began to feel like she'd made a bad decision.

She voiced these concerns to the lawyer Sue hired to make sure everything was legal and binding. Worried Mary would try and back out of their agreement, Sue came to the house and they created a solution.

Should Mary agree to give them three children, Sue would relinquish their care every summer. For two months the children would be Mary's. Sue would also sign over her share of the business and property the family owned. The only thing Sue demanded was Mary never tell the children the truth. Mary agreed, probably too quickly.

That was the last time Sue came into the house.

But Mary won in the end. She won a dozen summers

with her daughters, teaching them, watching them and giving them love.

As she grew to love the girls and understand how lucky they were to have three parents who cared for them, she came to a startling discovery. She did not want the life she led for them. She did not want them to become Keeper.

But...

It was too late. One day she realized the darkness had already tainted them and the oldest was destined to become Keeper of the Dead. So, she sent them away and told them never to return. She promised herself they would never come back and then they would be safe and free to live their lives unburdened.

But as Sue once learned, a promise like that is like a pie crust. Easily made and easily broken.

Love,
    Lorelei

"IS THAT IT? IT'S ALL TANGLED UP IN A STORY?" LOLA asked, disappointed.

"I don't think it's just a story. I think in every tale she spun Lorelei was trying to give us the truth without breaking a promise she made to Mom." Thana bit her lip, thinking.

"Why wouldn't Mom want us to know?" Lola asked

"Because she's a selfish bitch." Morana was back. She hopped off the bottom step and slammed the fridge door open. Popping a beer open, she took a long drink. The only sound in the room was the carbonated liquid being gulped down in a rush.

"She's not, don't say that. She and dad love us, they've done their best," Thana defended.

"What did she say?" Lola asked as she handed Morana her book. Morana put the beer down and wiped her hand on her jeans before accepting it. A look passed over her face Thana didn't understand.

"She wouldn't discuss it, said it was private business and Lorelei had no right to tell us, even post-mortem." Morana opened the book and read the information. Closing her eyes forcefully she shut the little blue book, gripping it so tightly that her fingers were leaving indents.

"What's wrong?" Thana asked. Stupid question…Of course, everything in that moment was wrong.

"We could have had a real mother. One who loved us and wanted to spend time with us. Instead, we got...her." So much anger tinted her words.

"Morana." Lola stood up and put arms around their little sister. "Mom loves us, she wanted us…she's just different from us. She gave us everything she could, including a relationship with Lorelei. She is our real mother."

"I can't forgive any of them. How could Lorelei have pushed us from the only home we'd ever had, especially if she loved us so much?" Tears were welling in Morana's deep blue eyes and starting to trickle down her face.

Guilt swelled up in Thana's stomach, causing nausea to burn in the back of her throat. It was her fault, she didn't know how or why, but she did know that it was her fault they'd been cast from Forgotten hills.

"It's my fault," the words were out of her mouth before she could stop them.

Her sisters turned to stare at her, mouths open.

"What?" Lola croaked.

"It's my fault she made us leave," Thana said, a sob rising in her voice.

"What did you do?" Morana's accusation stung, her eyes narrowing.

Thana opened her mouth and then shut it. It wasn't her secret to share. She'd promised Draven not to tell anyone.

Taking a deep breath, she made to speak again. Why was she still protecting a decade's old promise she'd made as a child? Her phone vibrated in her pocket.

"Don't answer it," Morana warned.

"I have to. It might be Dorian or the gravediggers." Reluctantly she took out her phone.

A simple text waited for her from Draven.

Tell them

Wide-eyed she looked around, toward the windows, but nothing greeted her but foliage. Straining she heard a creak from behind her, where the door to the hallway was, where it stood partially opened.

Her phone went off again.

I was coming to see you and heard your conversation. I'm sorry I eavesdropped. Tell them, Thana. It wasn't your fault, but mine.

She put the phone on silent, keeping it in her hand, within view.

Thana looked up at her sisters. "The year I was five I met a boy here. He was shy and quiet, and we became fast friends. He'd climb up and perch on the low wall near the ring."

Another deep breath in.

"I saw him every summer, as often as I could. The one thing he asked me was that I not tell anyone."

"You had a friend and we never knew?" Morana scoffed.

"Morana," Lola admonished. But Morana's tone was truthful. Thana never made friends as easily as Lola and Morana did.

"Why didn't he want you to tell us?" Lola asked, sitting back down, hands splaying over her own pink book.

"I never asked. As I got older, I got the impression his family life was bad, that maybe sneaking away to see me was a refuge."

Another text.

Too close to the truth. Why is it you see through me so easily?

"Of course, your one friend would be damaged. Wasn't there another broken little kid you hung out with in high school?" Morana asked.

"Beth…but that's not important…tell us what happened," Lola coaxed.

"That last summer, I'd started to see him as more than a friend. I was confused by how I felt. He'd never given the impression he liked me. I snuck off to see him, claiming I was grabbing the picnic basket."

Wrong

It was unnerving to know he was in the hall listening to every word she said.

"I remember that," Morana said. She got another beer from the fridge and sat next to Lola.

"We talked and for the first time ever he came down from the wall. We kissed and Lorelei caught us. She was furious. I don't know why, but afterward, she seemed sad and resigned. About a week after we came home Mom told us we wouldn't be going back…ever. I just knew it was my fault."

I'd never been kissed like that before. It was selfish of me. I knew she'd be angry.

"It doesn't sound like you did anything wrong. I'd love to be pissed and blame you, but that sounds like bunk," Morana said.

"Draven," Lola said.

Thana didn't look at her. She was looking at her phone.

"What about him?" Morana asked, leaning back in her chair.

"The boy," Lola said. She stood up and walked over to Thana.

Thana looked at her, hoping her expression was calm and gave nothing away.

"It was Draven, right?"

"Seriously? Weird eye boy?" Morana asked, barking out a laugh. "Priceless."

"Yes, it was Draven," Thana said. Her phone lit up again, incoming text message. Lola snatched it away before Thana could read it.

Lola stared at the words then her eyes went to the door behind Thana. Angry she stormed over and threw it all the way open, stalking inside the dim hallway.

She returned a few moments later. "Empty," she said and handed the phone back to Thana.

The text said:

It was always going to be me

EIGHTEEN

7 Months Earlier

LOLA CREPT DOWN THE STAIRS. IT WAS EARLY IN THE MORNING and she didn't want to wake Andrew. He'd gotten home late, done extra work and come to bed cranky and passed out. She was a little relieved. It meant he wouldn't try and pressure her to have sex with him.

She placed a hand on the slight swell of her belly and smiled. This child was the nicest and most beautiful thing Andrew had given her in three years. He'd also been treating her better since she announced they were having a baby. He lit up like a Christmas tree, took her to dinner, wrapped his arms around her and told her she and the baby were the most precious things he could ever be given.

She'd basked in his praise like she always did. But she knew his good mood wouldn't last. Eventually, he'd start calling her names again and complain about everything she did. If she was lucky, he wouldn't hit her until after the baby was born and honestly, she planned to be gone long before that happened.

"Miss Dolores?"

Lola paused on the bottom stair and looked at their maid, a sweet middle-aged woman who did their cooking and cleaning.

"I'm just going to drive out to the park for a walk," she said. Their code just in case Andrew woke up.

Esmeralda gave her a knowing smile anyway. "Your bags are in the trunk. I will remind him exercise is good for the baby." Esmeralda kept all of Lola's things at the bottom of her own closet.

"Thank you," Lola said and hurried toward the garage, grateful for Esmeralda. She didn't have her own car, so she could only use Andrew's on a quiet morning like this. He didn't like her to take public transportation or ride share services.

This was the only time she felt like herself, the ten-minute drive to the park, sitting in the leather seats, listening to old 90's songs on the radio. These few hours every month was the only respite she got from being the perfect wife and hostess. The only relief from keeping up the façade she and Andrew were madly in love and still happy.

That would all change soon. She was so close to her goal. A few hundred dollars more from her sewing and art and she could leave. Buy a cheap car, pack the things she really loved and go to Morana in Portland or Thana on the East Coast without being a burden to either of them.

She parked the sleek silver Mercedes and tugged on a bright pink wig and shivered under her coat. The large brown coat hid the thin pink homemade jumper, her normal disguise.

Getting out, she waved and smiled to the familiar faces at the craft fair. They didn't know her real name, so she felt comfortable being a friendly acquaintance to most.

Walking to her normal booth she began to unpack her boxes. Without the ability to sell her items online or take phone orders this was the only time she could sell. It had taken her a year to earn the amount a money currently sitting in her secret savings account. If Andrew ever caught on, if he ever found out…She trembled in the morning sunlight. She'd probably be dead or locked in her bedroom for the rest of her life.

"You could just call Thana and Morana. They'd come to get you," a voice in her mind said as she set out half a dozen hand painted scarfs and knitted hats with little flowers in a myriad of colors.

"I don't need rescuing. I can save myself and my baby," she whispered, knowing her pride was showing. She just didn't want to admit to her sisters how foolish she'd been. How for years she'd put up with Andrew's behavior, convinced it was her fault. She was embarrassed.

Lola hung up tie-dyed jumpers, paisley skirts, and a few odd sundresses. She put out the few drawings she'd done of local places and then put out the box of custom orders she'd taken last month.

"Oh, this is lovely!" A woman came up to the booth and began looking through her wares.

Lola smiled, blushing at the praise and finished putting up her sign.

Lorelei's Conceptions.

———

Lola, Morana and Thana stood around the little grave and looked at Dabria's coffin, alone six feet down in the ground.

Lola and Morana had done a good job clearing out all the tall grass and weeds. It was a simple little plot now with a stone wall six-foot-tall surrounding it and a cast iron gate with a padlock. The only key was on Thana's key ring; black and heavy. A constant reminder of Dabria.

The gravediggers stood around, awkwardly picking their nails and whispering among themselves after they lowered the casket in. The three girls stood in silence. Should they speak?

Something just felt wrong the entire time. It felt wrong when she pulled the forgotten coffin from storage and it felt wrong when she got Dabria from the freezer, cleaned her up, laid her in the ivory silk and put her in one of Lola's satin dresses, blue with pearl buttons. She looked so alive resting in her new home. Thana knew she was doing the right thing, wasn't she?

She spent the night before poring over her computer, torturing herself with articles about the Lottes. Fretting over her name when it appeared and praying she was making the right decision. She could see her name in the headlines now "Thana Muerticillo Caught with an Unknown Body in Freezer," "Mishandling of Remains at Forgotten Hills," "Mortician Forced to Sell Family Land to Pay Fines." She barely slept and when she finally woke up it was from nightmares about the Lottes sneering at her that she was no better than them.

She didn't tell anyone in town. She didn't tell Draven and the guilt over keeping it from him after she'd spent the last few nights in his arms, sneakily tucked against him on the couch in her office—was all consuming.

Lola was chipper this morning. In her eyes, this would put an end to everything that had gone wrong since they came back to Forgotten Hills, but Morana was hesitant, each day quieter and every morning tired.

The air around the grave was fresh. Smells of fall and the wind touched their hair and clothes in a lukewarm embrace.

Each sister lay a rose on Dabria's coffin. Thana said a few brief words. She didn't know what to say but she knew she had to say something. It wasn't right to lay a person to rest without wishes for a peaceful rest.

The three of them, dressed in whatever black clothing they could find, walked away as the gravediggers began covering her up.

"I'll give them a cash tip when they come back to the house," Thana told her sisters.

"Ummm, I think I'll take care of that. You'll be busy," Morana said, as they came through the trees and the porch became visible.

Standing on the front porch was Draven and he looked furious. His hair was mussed, and he was in a gray suit with a mint green shirt, looking handsome and professional.

"Is he mad at you? For what?" Lola asked. Her features were stiff as she observed him.

"It's fine. Don't worry Lola," Thana said. She put a hand on Lola's arm. She didn't want her worried and so far, the therapist and doctor she was seeing were happy with how well she was recovering.

"He doesn't have any right to be angry. This is your house and property." Lola's fists clenched at her sides.

"Just take her into the house, through the back. I'll meet you inside," Thana said to Morana.

"Okay, but don't take long. The reopening ceremony is in two weeks and we need to go over the menu, plus I need you to finalize the invitations," Morana reminded her.

Draven came down off the porch and stalked toward her.

"I know, I know, just go," Thana said. She watched as her sisters walked away and went through the cemetery gate.

"Thana, how could you?" Draven asked once he was within an arm's length of her.

"You knew I was considering it. I have inspectors coming in a few days. Not to mention I'm giving a tour to a few journalists to bring some positive publicity. She had to go. It wasn't right she was down there!"

"I told you not to disturb her. You have no idea what you've done. You need to put her back into the morgue before she thaws." Draven bit out each word, a hand running through his hair.

"How would I know what I've done when no one will tell me? I am in the dark like there's this awful secret lying around that affects my life, but no one will say what it is. I have done what I feel is best and if you don't like it..." she paused and took a breath in full of strength and courage she continued, "you can leave."

There, it was ugly and hateful, but it was out there. Draven reacted like she'd slapped him.

"Leave?" he asked, frowning. "Thana, how could I possibly leave here? Especially now?"

"Well, nothing is keeping you here, Draven. I've obviously done something unforgivable." Hands on her hips she stared up at him, heart aching. She'd let him get too close, this was obvious.

Draven looked to the sky. "Lorelei, forgive me," he whispered, then he reached out and gripped her shoulders and dragged her frame against him, wrapping his arms around her, lips in her hair whispering against her skin.

"Thana, the story she told you, about the woman who saved her town from the plague? It's true. Every single word of it."

Thana stiffened against him. "That's impossible."

Pulling away so he could tilt her face up he kissed her forehead and each eye. "It is, I swear it. This town only survived because of Dabria. I don't know what will happen now that you've put her back in the ground, but your aunt was convinced it would be horrible. The entire town believes this as well. You and your sisters will be in danger if anyone finds out."

"Let's say I believe this. Why not just tell me, why keep it a secret? Wouldn't it be safer if I knew?" Thana asked.

"The town protects themselves. They don't talk about Dabria to anyone. Only the current Keeper can talk about her. You have not accepted the position yet. Lorelei didn't want you to. I think she knew one day you'd have to come back. Who else could it be?" Draven explained.

"So, she hoped I'd just ignore the weird like I'd be unofficially Keeper of the Dead?"

"Yes, because once you accept your role here you won't ever leave. She wanted you to have whatever future you wanted. Even if you came back here, to be able to choose to leave again." Draven kissed her mouth gently, warm breath on her lips.

She pulled away. "I can leave whenever I want. I make my own choices, Draven. A stupid superstition and antiquated title won't change that."

"It will."

"I don't know what scares me more. The idea that it's true or that you and a whole town believe such nonsense," Thana said.

"Can you at least believe I won't leave here? I won't leave you?" He stroked a finger along her jawline.

"No," she whispered closing her eyes. After Dani, how could she trust him? He kept secrets too.

Feather light kisses touched her cheeks and then her lips. He raised her wrist and kissed a path over and around it.

"When you first arrived here, I wanted you to leave. Because your aunt wanted a different life for you. But even in the end, she knew you'd be Keeper of the Dead after her. She knew the legacy was safe. That either you or your sisters would provide the next. I was fighting a battle against myself and now I don't want to. You belong here at Forgotten Hills, Thana. Just as I do," his voice was hushed, his breath against her skin and his lips trailed across her collarbone and up her neck.

He raised his head and met her eyes, which were hooded and heavy with desire. Why did she feel like this? With him? It would be so much easier to push him away. To believe there was something wrong with him and with how he made her feel.

She swallowed, mouth dry like she'd eaten a cup of sand or forgotten water after smoking a joint.

"You wanted me to leave," she pointed out.

"Not anymore. I told you. Have you always been this stubborn?" He touched a finger to the tip of her nose.

"Always," she said, mouth betraying her into a smile.

"You should leave and never come back. Things are about to spiral out of control here and I worry for you," he said.

"But…"

"But I don't want you to go. I shouldn't have let Lorelei send you away that summer. I should have dragged you back here with me after our first time together." His forehead touched hers as a cool breeze wrapped around them making her remember she wasn't dressed properly to be outside for so long. The black collared shirt was thin, and her deep purple pencil skirt didn't protect her legs from the slight chill in the air.

Next time she had an impromptu funeral in the woods she'd need to remember leggings or tights. The thought made her chuckle. Draven raised an eyebrow and she shrugged. It wasn't interesting enough to explain.

"You couldn't have argued with her. You were fifteen too, and if you'd brought me back here, she would have been furious. I needed to live my life and you yours." She settled for simply continuing their conversation.

"I care about you and Forgotten Hills. I care about your sisters too, your whole family. Only once has anyone ever treated me close to how you do," he said, wrapping an arm around her shoulders. They walked together back to the front porch.

"You've given me a headache, Draven. I don't know what to do, say or believe."

She rubbed her temples, exhausted and it was only noon. He was either nuts or she'd stepped in something much more awful than anything she'd dealt with before. Neither thought was comforting.

"Save that excuse for later," he teased.

Raising up on tiptoes to kiss him again, she stopped, hearing a vehicle approaching. Putting back on her business appropriate expression she watched as a sleek white town car came slowly down the driveway.

Draven took a step away from her, standing stiffly by her side. She looked at him questioningly.

The car parked in front of Forgotten Hills and the driver got out. He was ridiculously handsome, with chiseled features, a narrow nose and wide mouth. His eyes were sparkling blue and his hair so blonde it was white. He wore a black suit, so tailored it had to be custom, with a crisp white shirt and gold tie.

Smiling he came around the porch and mounted the steps.

"Good day! When I heard they were reopening Forgotten Hills, I had to come to see myself. It's been such a long time since I visited Hill City," he said, voice deep.

"Cessair, what are you doing here?" Draven asked. Everything about him screaming this man was unwanted.

"Draven forgets his manners." Cessair held out a perfectly manicured hand. "Cessair..." he paused and looked at Draven, chuckling, "of course...Cessair Smith."

"Oh, you're Draven's brother?" Thana asked, she reached

out to shake his hand, but Draven snaked an arm out stopping her.

"Draven!" she admonished. Why was he being so rude?

"No, it's okay. I can understand Draven's hesitation. I haven't seen him in a very long time," Cessair said, his smile getting wider with every second.

"Cessair," Draven growled.

"Oh, fine. Draven, the family is getting together this weekend, dinner in Portland. You should come and bring this," he looked down his nose at Thana, "charming? Yes, that's the right word, this charming lady with you. I'm sure our sisters would love her."

Thana bristled. He might be Draven's brother, but they were like night and day. While Draven was quiet and sincere if not confusing, Cessair was an entitled ass. She looked down at herself and wondered if she weren't the type of girl Draven normally dated, or maybe Cessair didn't know him well enough to judge his girlfriends?

"I'm Thana Muerticillo. It's been a pleasure meeting you, but if you don't have any business here, I think it's time you left. As you can tell we're not open for business yet," Thana said, using her best boss bitch voice.

"Thana Muerticillo? Ah, Lorelei's niece. The little girl from the cemetery all those years ago. I understand now why Draven has stuck around Hill City so long," he said. He glanced around the building, taking in the updates and upgrades.

"You seem to be doing a good job here. It did so need a new coat of paint, but as I said it's been what feels like centuries since I was here last. Nothing interesting ever really happens here," he said laughing. Reaching in his back pocket he took out a brown leather wallet and dipped his long thin fingers inside, caressing it.

He took out a business card and handed it to her.

"With a new building and additions comes the need for many new things, like insurance, advertising and," he glanced at the woods, "a realtor. All of which my company does. I am good at my job. In fact, I could sell water to a fish." His grin showed all his straight perfect teeth.

"Thank you, Mr. Smith. I'll keep you in mind if I decide to change insurance agencies," Thana said.

"Draven, I'll call you about dinner. Hopefully you'll come. One should get over old grudges." Cessair turned and began back to his car.

"I have no issue with our sisters," Draven called after him. Cessair paused for just an instant, tension in his body. Then he got in his fancy car and drove away.

"I'll share my sisters with you any day," Thana said, hugging Draven to her. He still hadn't moved and every inch of him radiated with irritation.

The business card fell to the ground. She looked down and read the card:

Curse the Competition with
Bane Industries

NINETEEN

THERE WERE RULES AT AUNT'S LORELEI'S HOUSE. THEY weren't written down and sometimes they changed. New ones popped up, old outdated ones disappeared, but the girls had them memorized.

1) Dinner together every night

2) No playing in the cemetery after dark

3) No apologizing—unless it was for something serious, important and your apology was truthful.

4) If your clothes got grass stains on them throw them out. Lorelei hates laundry.

5) Morana isn't allowed to be around anything scary.

6) We don't use Lola's real name on vacation.

7) Thana's the big sister, but during the summer she's not your babysitter, not your source of entertainment and not your mom—figure things out yourself.

8) Bathroom time is private time. If you really can't hold it, use the one in the funeral parlor.

9) Try something new every summer.

10)You're not allowed in the basement without supervision.

11) We call Mom every Sunday night.

12) Except when we're hot, hungry, tired or on an adventure, then screw calling Mom.

13) Don't flush the tampons.

14) Clean up your cooking messes, especially if they explode all over the oven.

15) Count your needles. What comes out of the basket goes back in the basket. No one wants to sit on or step on a sewing needle.

Some were girl specific, others not so much. One summer they broke every single rule and Lorelei made them eat borsht for dinner for a week as punishment. Thana couldn't believe how many different types of beets there were, or how even the pretty ones still tasted like spoiled dirt.

The rule that got broken the most was 5. Thana loved scary movies and scary stories, Lola tolerated them well enough, but she'd rather have a mystery or a romance. They compromised with scary mysteries. Morana was little, she liked funny things and cartoons. She never grew out of this fascination and had a tattoo of Mickey Mouse on her right hip.

One night after they thought Morana went to bed they indulged in a favorite pastime. Asking their aunt for a story.

"Tell us a story now that she's in bed," Thana begged, she was 13.

"Yes, but not too scary," Lola warned.

Their aunt was on the couch with them, working on embroidery. She stopped what she was doing and looked at them with serious eyes.

The girls wore matching white nightgowns with their initials sewn into the collars. After their showers scrubbed them clean, Lorelei always painted their toes and braided their hair.

She put her sampler down and smiled at them. "I guess

that's ok, as Morana is in her room."

"Yes!" Thana exclaimed and scooted closer to her sister.

"There is a woman who is dead but not. She sleeps the death-like sleep. No air fills her lungs and no blood pulses through her veins. She is dead and she died for a good cause, but to say she is always dead or dead in the way others are is a lie. She can wake. Oh not in her body, but her spirit can wake. If she is ever disturbed and her spirit roused from its slumber, she will come back a terrifying specter. Her spirit will detach from the physical vessel that binds it and will be an angry, vengeful thing, spewing its wrath on those she deems deserve it. Nothing can reason with such an angry ghost. She will hold on to her last memory of life."

"What is her last memory?" Thana asked, eyes wide.

"Of a man, of course. A man who she took to her bed only once. He will become her soul's focus and nothing else will soothe her back into her body and allow her to rest once more."

"Where is her body now?" Lola asked.

"I'd like to tell you buried far from here, alas this is not true. She is," Lorelei paused and then reached out and grabbed them, "in our basement!"

Both girls screamed and then began to laugh, but their laughter cut off as they heard crying. Lorelei got up and looked behind the couch frowned and leaned over, scooping up a terrified and tiny six-year-old Morana.

"Oh darling, we're so sorry, we thought you went to bed," Lorelei cooed and hushed, rocking their sister. Wide eyed and weeping, Morana clutched her My Little Pony coloring book to her chest.

Morana slept on the end of Lola's bed for a week and made her keep two-night lights on.

———

Thana held a letter in her hand and groaned. Another letter? Maybe this time it could contain good news? A happy fairytale where everyone lives a normal and pleasant life? She doubted it.

Draven presented her with this letter two days after Dabria's burial and the strange visit from his brother. It was the last thing Lorelei ever wrote for her, to be read if Thana decided not to listen to the other notes of warning and Draven's insistence she not meddle.

"If I ever have children, I won't leave them with some cryptic crap. I will just tell them how fucking crazy our family is," she said. Draven was sitting across from her in the office. He was drinking coffee, black, while hers had a heavy dose of steamed milk and sugar.

"Have you told your sisters?" he asked.

"What, that a dead girl is haunting us? The town might descend upon us with some awful curse and our relative had sex with death to bring back her dead baby? Ummm, let me think…no."

Draven remained silent and Thana rolled her eyes. "Yeah, yeah, I get it. Lorelei was trying to protect me from the crazy,"—she pointed a finger at him—"crazy I don't fully believe."

"Had you listened to me and believed her warnings you could have lived here in ignorance until you died and passed on your trade to the next generation," Draven pointed out.

"Did you really believe that would happen?"

"No. I hoped for it, but no. I felt Lorelei deserved a chance to do things her way. She knew if she failed, there had to be a backup plan. This letter and me."

"Okay, here we go." Thana ripped the envelope open.

Querida,
    If you are reading this all my plans to keep you unaware

have failed and Draven believes you should know the truth. I know you, my sweet thing. You've disturbed Dabria, uncovered the truth surrounding your life and are now thinking I was batshit crazy.

If I could, I'd spin this truth into another story for you, but I can no longer do so. I have given you all the puzzle pieces. Your mother forbade me from telling you anything about your heritage or how you and your sisters came to be. I can honestly say I kept that promise. If this letter has reached you, I am dead and so cannot be held to a promise I made decades ago, while alive.

There is a box buried in the ring that holds the original death records from the plague as well other documents that might be important should the worst come to pass. You must wait until the moon is high and the light will shine and show you where to dig. I apologize in advance for sending you into the cemetery during the night. Our ancestors didn't have any foresight.

Ah, the rest. My darling, we are the descendants of the child that Dabria's sacrifice brought back from the dead. As far as I can tell none of her other children had progeny, or if they did, they escaped our blessing. Yes, it is a blessing. We are Keepers of the Dead, protectors of our small town. Dabria gave a great gift to the people living here and to us. We are alive because of her sacrifice. Should her death be disturbed that protection will end.

Your birthmark is a binding symbol that you have already been touched by death and are safe from harm. Not death or its relations can harm you or your sisters.

Before I go you must consider these last words. If Dabria is awakened, she will be an angry and hungry ghost clinging to the last memories of her life on earth. You will not be able to use her to save the people of Hill City again. You will have to find.another.way.

Love,
   Lorelei

"You're shitting me." Thana put the letter down, running a finger over Lorelei's signature, a pang in her chest letting her know that even with all the insanity above it, how much she needed to see those words in writing, from Lorelei.

"I know it's difficult to believe, but you are living in a town where everyone believes this, where we all grow up knowing this tale is true. Your family is revered through town and spoken of in hushed whispers. They pray for your safety."

"That doesn't make me feel any better, Draven."

Thana sat back and then shook her head. "I can't believe this stuff. It's impossible. I don't even believe in God!"

"God and death are not remotely the same thing," Draven told her.

"Okay, I'll go out into the cemetery and get the records, but until I have more proof than a loony old lady's letters, I'm not taking any of this at face value."

"Don't go without me," Draven warned.

Before she could argue with him there was a knock at the office door. Thana hid the letter. "Come in!"

Lola was on the other side, nervous. "That old lady, Mrs. Gilhoulie, she's here and she's really upset. She doesn't look good either."

"Did Dorian show up to finish the painting and bring the gardener I asked about?" Thana asked, standing up.

"Yes, Morana fed them a whole apple pie and they went to work," Lola said, laughing.

"Okay, I'll take care of Mrs. Gilhoulie. What are your plans for today?"

"I think I'm going to start selling some of my items online. I think I could make a small profit from that," Lola said.

"Good idea. Between that and the money your douchebag ex is going to have to pay out, you are going to be fine." Thana hugged her sister proud of her.

"My lawyer is trying to make it so I don't have to go to court, but..."

"It might make you feel better to go and have a chance to confront him, in a way," Thana finished.

"Yeah. I left her on the porch." Lola went back toward the kitchen.

Thana went out and opened the large front doors. Dorian had convinced her to replace them with something brighter and newer. Now they were a beige oak with designs carved around small glass windows. She was glad he'd convinced her to change them.

They were done with the paint on the outside. She'd chosen a dark teal with hints of gray for the borders and brighter teal with a bit more green for the walls, trying to mimic the old shade without it being so vintage. It looked nice.

As she glanced around the large porch, she made a mental note to buy some outdoor furniture.

Mrs. Gilhoulie sat on the front steps, hunched over and coughing into a handkerchief. The old woman seemed thinner and frailer than she had the last time Thana saw her. She looked up at Thana and there were sores around her mouth. Her eyes were red and watery. Her hat skewed on her head. The buttons on her flowered shirt weren't done right and her gray cotton pants were stained. From the smell of her, not just with dirt or food.

The old lady hacked into the white kerchief again and shakily stood up. She pointed a wrinkled finger at Thana, accusation in her eyes and stance. Her hands were covered in a red rash.

"You! I told you, foolish, stupid girl, not to mess around

with Dabria. I went by her grave, I know what you've done." She took in a wheezing breath, spittle around her mouth, sweat beads forming on her upper lip.

"The whole town is going to suffer for this, selfish, senseless child. I told Lorelei she should have given you the truth, but she ignored me and now we are all going to die!"

"Mrs. Gilhoulie, you don't look well. Maybe I should take you to the doctor?" Thana stepped forward, but the old lady stepped back, almost falling as she gasped for air. She put her hand to her chest, coughing into her covered hand again. This time Thana could tell there was blood on the white cloth.

"And you! You are letting her do this. You want us all to finally die!" Her hoarse yell was directed at Draven.

"Mrs. Gilhoulie, I thought you didn't know Draven?" Thana got out her cell phone, ready to call 911.

"Draven?" She chuckled darkly bringing on another coughing fit. She spat blood on the ground.

It wasn't a nice thought, but Thana made another mental note; bleach, lots of bleach and disinfectant.

"Is that what he's calling himself these days?" Mrs. Gilhouile gasped, struggling for each breath.

Draven took a step toward Mrs, Gilhoulie. "Call 911," he told Thana and reached out to steady Mrs. Gilhoulie who looked about to fall over.

"Don't touch me!" the old woman screamed, but it was too late. Draven's hand connected with her elbow to steady her.

Mrs. Gilhoulie keeled over in a dead faint; Draven caught her before she hit the ground.

"Is she dead?" Thana asked, phone against her ear as she called for an ambulance.

"No, but I think she will be," Draven said.

TWENTY

IT WAS HOURS BEFORE THANA AND DRAVEN HAD ANY downtime. Mrs. Gilhoulie was taken away by ambulance and the paramedics didn't look hopeful that she'd even make the ride to the hospital.

The sheriff stopped by to take their statements and to lecture Thana about her hateful and careless actions. Thana found herself promising to put Dabria back in the morgue just to appease the angry white man with easy access to a rifle. He didn't know that at this point it was useless, but she was scared that the entire community would appear on her porch to tar and feather her if she wasn't careful.

What she didn't want was for this to affect the reopening of Forgotten Hills, and she really didn't want her first job to be someone killed by her actions. If that's what was truly going on. Logical, rational Thana knew magic, curses, and ghost didn't exist, but slowly that part of her was being taken over by what she was seeing and feeling.

Several town's residents called and left nasty voicemails and both her sisters were verbally accosted when they went into town for groceries. Thana had to do something. These people were begging to be saved. They wanted Thana and her sisters to fix what happened.

"They are all crazy assholes, thinking we caused this sickness to spread," Morana said, angry and stomping through the kitchen. She slammed a gallon of milk on the counter.

"They're scared, Morana. They all believe burying Dabria caused the plague to come back. We have to help them," Lola spoke to Morana, but her eyes were for Thana.

"Superstitious idiots, what do they expect us to do? Magically pull a cure out of our asses?"

"Well, that would be colorful, but not quite what they have in mind," Thana said, then she laughed and felt bad about it.

"Help me put the groceries away, Morana, then you can make me some Budin de Pan," Lola said. She began unloading a purple reusable bag.

"You want bread pudding?" Morana asked.

"You always feel better when you bake," Thana said. "I'm going upstairs. Be right back."

She changed as soon as she got to her room, into jeans and a deep purple peasant blouse she found in her aunt's closet, taking strength in the scent that lingered on the fabric. Then she went back into the mortuary to find Draven in her office. As soon as the door closed his arms wrapped around her and for a few minutes she forgot about illnesses, secrets and ghosts. For just a blink in time it was just her and him. Heat, passion and comfort.

When their furious make out session was done Draven helped her straighten her blouse.

"I love it best when you look like this," he said.

"Disheveled and flushed?" she asked, putting her hair into a messy bun.

"No, like yourself."

He put his hands on each side of her face. He pulled her down into another mind-numbing kiss.

Draven left the house a little after seven with the promise to come back first thing in the morning, even if it was a Saturday. She watched him walk away and disappear around the cemetery wall.

One day she'd make him take her back to his house. Though she was afraid that it would be a one-room shack or such a bachelor's pad she'd run screaming. She once dated a man who lived in a studio apartment. Every surface was covered in unopened mail, dust, and empty beer bottles. The bed was a bare mattress on the floor, but his closet meticulous and color coded.

She watched the sunset. In Hill City sunsets were different than anywhere else. The pale blue sky slowly went away as sienna, magenta, and chiffon melded together on the horizon and bled to a greenish black.

Around the mortuary and into the cemetery the blue-green twilight flowed over the land, throwing shades and making the already beautiful view downright mystical and scary.

"What are you doing out here?" Lola came up behind her, leaning on the railing looking out. Her hair loose and flowing around her shoulders, ashen in the lack of light.

"You'll get cold," Thana cautioned. Lola still wore her black funeral clothes. Leggings and a short-sleeved tunic striped in black and white.

"Nah, but you didn't answer my question."

"I'm watching nightfall."

"That's not all you're doing. I know you too well."

"I found another letter from Lorelei," Thana admitted, staring up as the sky darkened and small flicks of bright white flickered on overhead.

"That woman and her letters."

Lola's laughter broke the silence of nightfall.

"She says there are some records buried in the ring and the moonlight will show me where to dig."

"No way. We don't go into the cemetery at night," Lola said. She shook her head and reached a hand out, gripping Thana's arm.

"As soon as the moon rises, I'm going," she tried to project more confidence than she felt. A small shovel leaned against the cemetery gate as well as a flashlight. The dark metal shadows reminding her of an unwanted task.

"What did Draven say? Why isn't he going with you?"

"I don't need Draven's help or permission," Thana said, bristling. She looked at Lola and raised an eyebrow.

Lola flinched and blushed. "Sorry, old habits die hard."

"Don't apologize. You aren't there anymore, and you don't say you're sorry unless it's important and true." One of their summertime Lorelei rules.

Lola grinned and her shoulders stiffened. "Then I'm coming with you."

"No."

"I am. No way are you going in alone."

"Lola, there are things I haven't told you."

"That there is a ghost girl haunting us? I'm not Morana and scared of everything, but I do have eyes."

Sometimes Lola still surprised her.

While they talked the moon rose high in the sky, shining silvery light on the house and grounds. A comforting wash of light over the darkness.

"Okay, let's go." Thana stepped off the porch and went to the gate, gravel noisy beneath her booted feet.

Lola grabbed the flashlight and Thana got the shovel. She opened the gate and they stepped into the cemetery.

For a moment everything was quiet, but it felt like stepping into a different world. The moonlight barely illuminated the path and everywhere they looked held shadows and darkness.

Lola jumped when Thana closed and locked the gate

behind them, the loud clank and rattle deafening in the silence.

"Is the back door unlocked?" Lola whispered.

"Yes, why are you whispering?" Thana whispered back. They gave each other nervous grins and Lola turned the flashlight on.

Fake yellow light lit up the path and drove some gloom back.

"We should install outdoor lights," Lola commented as they began walking the familiar route.

"Already ahead of you, I texted Dorian about it an hour ago." Thana was distracted. The further into the graveyard they got the more she noticed the sounds.

Not the normal sounds of wind through trees and bushes, or birdsong like during the day. A whispering, muttering sound. As if someone from very far away was talking, but she couldn't make out any words.

"Maybe Morana has the TV on and a window open?" Lola asked.

"I doubt it. Let's just get this over with." Thana gripped the shovel with two hands, knowing it would only be a good weapon against a physical threat.

As they got closer to the ring the muttering was louder and now it sounded like multiple people, but she still had to strain to make it out and she didn't understand it.

They came around the corner and for a moment it looked like the ring was full of people, but as the flashlight beam settled on the headstones, in the blink of an eye, it was empty and dark, and the whole place was silent, unnervingly so.

"Ummm, did you see that?" Lola asked. She stood very still, refusing to go any farther.

"I don't know what I saw and I'm planning to ignore it for now." Thana moved forward leaving Lola behind her. A cold crept along her spine until it felt like electricity over her skin and shoulders. She passed into the circle of headstones and every instinct in her body screamed at her to turn around and leave.

"We're being watched," Lola said. She'd moved a few feet closer and was swinging the flashlight in every direction.

"Stop that. Do you really want to see what's watching us? Let me do this and we'll run for the back door," Thana said. She stood in the center and looked at the ground.

The moonlight shone straight down, illuminating one headstone more than the others. Thana knelt and began to dig. The ground was soft and smelled like rich, healthy earth. Grass came up in clumps, green and stiff.

Her hands turned brown as she dug down, grit under her fingernails and then the shovel's tip hit something hard. Using her hands, she cleared the area and pulled out a metal box, not locked. A gray square box. The kind you keep money in at bake sales and school fundraisers.

"Got it," Thana said, getting to her feet. She'd fix the hole in the daylight.

The uncomfortable sensations ceased as she moved outside the ring and she took a deep breath in and handed the box to Lola.

From the corner of her eye she saw something streak toward her, white and gray. She almost didn't see it.

She spun quickly, but not fast enough and the thing hit her with a force she didn't understand as whatever it was wasn't solid.

"Thana!" Lola screamed.

She felt something leaving burning scratches down her arms, but aside from wisps of color, she couldn't make out what was attacking her. Fear and frustration filled every pore. Fight and flight responses battled in her mind as she hit the ground, trying to escape whatever it was attached to her. A low wail filled her ears and the cemetery.

"What should I do?" Lola yelled. Thana could see her moving frantically to help her.

"Stop," Thana said. She tried to hold out her hand but couldn't as invisible pressure held her down, panic rising in her throat.

Mine, mine, mine mine! The words hissed around her. Thana closed her eyes and Lola screamed again, in terror. Thana opened them and gasped, air locked in her throat.

A ghostly figure had her pinned down, long hair flowing around as if in a windstorm. Eyes like black burning holes in her face, lips back in a sneer and her face gaunt, nothing like the woman she remembered.

"Dabria," Lola choked out.

Leave here! You are trespassing on what's mine! The apparition shrieked in her face.

Pain radiated through Thana's side as Dabria sunk ghostly fingers into her flesh, mouth straining into a large grin.

Thana turned her head to see her sister was frozen, flashlight pointed at them, crying. Lola had no idea what to do, but Thana could tell she wasn't about to leave.

"I can't leave if you don't get off me," Thana ground out. She wasn't sure if sassing a ghost was a good idea, but at this point anything was better than succumbing to the terror and pain radiating through her body. Was she going to die here?

MINE! HE IS MINE! Dabria keened, digging her hands in further.

"Dabria, stop!"

Thana and Dabria looked up simultaneously. Time seemed to freeze. Draven was perched on the low wall. He was in black pajama bottoms and no shirt. His pale skin gleaming in the moonlight, eyes furious and mouth turned down into a frown.

"Thank God, Draven!" Lola exclaimed, a testimony to how frightened she was.

He jumped down, bare feet hitting the ground with a solid thump.

You dare? The words rustled around them.

"Let her go now. You aren't yourself, Dabria," he said, calmly walking toward them.

NO! She cried out and Thana heard the same hushed voices as before, even more of them and close.

"Oh my God," Lola moaned.

"Your family is going to be very cross with you if you hurt the current Keeper," Draven said. Slowly he knelt beside Thana, hands reaching out for her. The moment Dabria looked away Draven grabbed Thana and wrenched her from the spirit. Thana winced, shuddering in pain. Draven pulled her into his arms.

Dabria turned back to look at them and something akin to hurt glimmered in her black eyes as she slowly dissipated, and the cemetery went quiet once again.

"You couldn't wait for me? Just one night?" Draven asked kissing her forehead. "Stubborn woman."

Thana looked at Lola, both trembling.

Lola opened her mouth to speak and what she said next was not what Thana expected.

"Whatever you do, Thana, do not tell Morana. She'll sleep at the foot of my bed for a week."

TWENTY-ONE

Aunt's Lorelei's house had its own music at night. Like it was breathing in contented sighs. The smells of the day petered off to let in crisp night air flooded with the cemetery's rich wet scent, underneath a still dryness that tingled her nose.

Thana kept her window open so she could feel the night. Her room got stuffy sometimes and the window unit in the living room didn't reach her room.

She hated the room, with the beige walls and forest green carpet. Hated was a strong word. Not hated, it bored her. Her sisters had better rooms. Thana didn't begrudge them, she was the oldest and honestly, she felt as if all Forgotten Hills was hers. From the small closet where the water heater lived to the great expanse of woods and the lush green graveyard. If she could lay claim to all that wonder, then it was only right her room be boring.

The full-size bed had a black comforter and purple sheets. Her stuffed bat Reaper, worn from long nights of cuddling, lived there contently watching over the room. An old brown desk with a plush maroon chair was squished into one corner and a dresser in the other. One rickety bookshelf touched the bottom of her bed crammed with the twenty or so novels she always kept at Forgotten Hills.

Beloved classics like Little Women, Jane Eyre, Anne of Green Gables and the Oz books, along with some slim trashy Harlequin romance novels.

She sat on the edge of her bed, face as close to the window as she could get, wrapped in a black fluffy robe that felt like bunny fur and flowers. It had her name sewn in the side in neon purple thread. A gift from Lola this past Christmas.

It was 3 a.m., an unusual time to be awake, even for her. Thana loved the night, loved how everything changed color.

Her sisters and aunt were asleep. She could hear Lola's snores through the thin walls. Knew if she opened the door and tiptoed into the living room, she'd find Lorelei, not in her cozy bed, but asleep on the couch, reruns of Golden Girls playing on the old TV with the crooked antenna.

She thought about today and how angry her aunt was after finding her with Draven. She thought about his goodbye and a sense of sadness welled up in her chest. It was an eternal sadness, one she felt would never leave her.

Acknowledging her feelings were being caused by her teenage hormones did not make her feel any better.

From this window, she could crawl onto the porch roof and sit, if she wanted. But the shingles dug into skin unforgivingly and, unlike other roof angles, she'd be visible to all. She could see the cemetery wall, gate and all the driveway.

Staring into the night until her vision went blurry, she saw something. Blinking rapidly she brought a figure into focus, a pale slim form coming from the darkness.

She sat in disbelief, heart pounding in her chest as the figure got clearer and she saw it was Draven. Could he see her? The lights were off in her room, nothing but the small red illumination from her clock radio.

He began to run toward the house, keeping to the deepest shadows until he reached the porch. She leaned forward, heart in her throat now, eyes wide trying to see him better.

Then he was on the roof, silent as a thief. She froze, listening, her aunt surely had to hear him climb up, but there was nothing. The normal sounds of Forgotten Hills distant in her ears as her blood rushing replaced them.

When he reached her open window, he sat in front of it, watching her with his odd eyes, a slight smile on his face.

"What are you doing here?" she whispered, leaning toward him, moths fluttered in her stomach.

"I had to see you," he said. She flinched at how loud his voice sounded.

"If she catches you here…" she warned.

"She won't," he assured her. He reached through the window and touched her face.

"Promise you won't forget me," he demanded suddenly.

"That could never happen. Can I give you my address, my phone number?" She couldn't believe she'd never thought to exchange information with him before.

"I won't be able to write or call. I wish I could," he said, wistfully.

"I won't see you again, will I?" She tried to swallow past the lump in her throat.

"I don't know, maybe. Perhaps I'll just be like that story Lorelei tells you. The one about the widow and death, ships passing for a common goal," he said, laughing softly.

"I love that story. I can't believe you know it too."

"It's very popular around here. A woman who has sex with death to save an entire town? Almost romantic." Linking his fingers through hers, he drew them past the window barrier and rubbed each one. A tingle ran over her skin, heat flushing through her.

"What would a night with death be like?" Thana was never afraid to ask Draven questions, even the dark questions.

"I don't know. Would you like to find out some day?" he asked, grinning at her.

Feeling brave she crawled half out the window, shocking him. She pressed her mouth to his, wanting to taste him one last time, to know what it would be like.

"Maybe."

Two weeks later the result was seven deaths including Mrs. Gilhoulie and the Sheriff. Thana counted it lucky that so far, no children were affected, but now she knew all the suffering in town was her fault.

They were also lucky the town hadn't turned on them. She'd had several people come to her angry, sad, sick and despondent, but they seemed to believe her when she said she would fix things. The belief in her family and her ability to right this wrong and protect them all was more tangible than their anger, it appeared.

It also helped that she looked so wretched. Whatever Dabria's ghost had done, it didn't want to heal. She was pale, tired and had fingertip shaped bruises where the ghost dug into her skin. Scratches that wouldn't heal were hidden under her clothes and her whole body ached. Draven watched her with careful, guarded eyes.

The only positive thing was her inspections went well and she had all the proper permits and signatures in place, so she could open and operate. She had been right on that account, at least. If even a hint of something weird had been sniffed out, she wouldn't be opening.

Every person she encountered knew her reputation, that she'd been employed by the Lottes and even though she hadn't done anything wrong—they all treated her like she had. She was exhausted from the few days of hoop jumping just to get everything in place.

She wished she'd been wrong though. Being able to listen to Draven and her aunt's warnings would have been helpful because now she knew for certain she'd unleashed something awful into the world. The worst part was that she couldn't figure out how to fix it. She wasn't Dabria, a handy-dandy death man hadn't shown up in town and offered a means of escape.

She also didn't know what to do about the angry ghost haunting her. Dabria was disturbed. They couldn't reset her like a phone.

She was sitting against Elder, deep in thought about the state of things when she heard voices and footsteps.

Looking up she saw both her sisters. Morana had her make up on, wearing a jean jumper with a thin long sleeve blue shirt under it. Lola was in gray slacks and a cream-colored cardigan, hair in double braids, holding a picnic basket.

"What's up, sis?" Morana asked.

"Just thinking about things," she answered. She and Lola hadn't told her about the night in the cemetery or the curse on the town.

"You look sick. Are you getting enough sleep? I know you haven't been eating," Morana scolded.

"Sleep isn't the problem," Thana said, and it wasn't. She slept like the dead.

"Then you need more food!" Morana's fix for every problem; feed it.

Lola took out sandwiches Morana must have made.

Everyone knew Lola didn't cook, she burned. Alongside the sandwiches were homemade sweet potato chips and pickles.

Grateful, stomach growling to remind her how long it had been since she ate last, she grabbed a sandwich and bit into a pimento cheese filling that made her feel ten again.

"Yeah, I've been thinking too. I think I'm going back to Portland. Whatever illness has infected this town, I can't get it. I can't leave Trixie as a single mom. I also cannot deal with one more crying or sick person pleading with me to help them. The whole town is nuts," Morana said. She looked upset and worried.

Thana wasn't surprised. She considered telling them both to leave, but she knew that they were safe from the disease, and only them. She'd tried to get Draven to go, but he was a tenacious mule.

Morana licked her fingers as she polished off a sour pickle spear and Lola gave them each a water bottle filled with Morana's famous cumber and basil infused water.

Lola grabbed a bottle. Reaching in the pocket of her trousers, she pulled out a few pills and swallowed them all at once. She handed the remaining to Thana with a look. Thana obeyed and took the painkillers.

"I think that's a good idea. Isn't Trixie supposed to pop next month anyway?" she asked, nudging her sister with a bare toe. Morana sat in the only shaft of warm sunlight to filter between Elder's dead branches.

"Yes, and I miss her. I've left all the food for your party in the freezer with instructions," Morana said. "Now try and convince Lola to come with me!"

Thana leveled a gaze at her sister. Lola seemed sturdier recently. She'd been speaking to a lawyer and a psychologist and seeing a physical therapist for her arm. The circles under her eyes were lighter and all that was left of her brutal fall down the stairs were some winces, aches and one yellowing bruise, so sickly looking it wouldn't leave her collarbone.

"I think Morana's got a good idea."

Lola cleaned up their lunch, packing all garbage back into the basket.

"Nope, not going anywhere. I planned to make this my home until I feel safe again and that's exactly what I'm going to do." She crossed her arms under her breasts.

"You sure?" Thana asked and Lola nodded, slowly, seriously. This caused all three sisters to laugh.

"Okay, then I'm going to rent a car back to Portland and leave asap. Let me know if you change your mind." Morana stood up, dusted grass off her outfit and left their tiny hill.

"No way am I leaving you here with all the crazy," Lola said before Thana could open her mouth.

"Fine, then any ideas?"

"Did you look through the lockbox yet?"

"No." Thana brushed a hand down her side, pinching the green linen dress covering her skin, covering the ghost marks.

She'd had a hell of a time explaining them to Morana. A combination of working in the cemetery and rough sex with Draven seemed to convince her.

"They buried it for a reason," Lola admonished. Reaching back in the basket she pulled out the box.

"Lola!"

"What? I put it in there after Morana packed everything. Now open it."

Taking a deep breath, Thana grabbed the box and opened it. She gripped a thick plastic bag and poured out a dozen items; black and white pictures printed on heavy stock and documents yellow with time, many faded and brittle.

Delicately she pulled out an official list.

"Okay, here's what Lorelei wanted me to see. A list of the

people who died in the first outbreak. Names, dates of birth and death...wait." She saw something as she read the names.

"What?"

"Here, look at this. Tell me I'm crazy." Thana handed it to her. Lola spent a while longer reading and the cute frown lines on her forehead and between her eyes deepened with each passing minute.

"Everyone who has died now is related to someone who died then," Lola said, handing the paperwork back.

"Yes, and if the story is true all those people came back from the dead after Dabria died."

Lola shivered and looked around. "It's hard to be out here."

"It's daylight. I'm not afraid. But you bet your ass the moment the sun starts setting I'm out of here." Thana could understand Lola's apprehension, but nothing was going to scare Thana from her cemetery.

Thana dug through more documents, sneezing as dust rose. The old paper had a musty smell. She could tell it'd been a very long time since someone opened it last.

"Hey, I know this symbol." She drew out a hand-written note. On the top, she saw the divided circle, the strange marking on Dabria's hip.

"I've never seen anything like that before. I mean close... but not quite." Lola squinted at it.

It was hard reading the old hand-written note bu— "I think it's some sort of summoning spell?"

"Spell-like magic? Come on, that's crap," Lola said, eyes raising with doubt.

Thana gave her serious eyes. "Like ghosts and disease curses?" Her sister went silent.

"Looks like the guy, death, whatever Dabria fucked that saved the whole town told her daughter how to summon him again if she ever needed him and these are the instructions," Thana said.

"Is that a good idea?"

"If I don't do something this whole town will die and it's my fault. The only thing I can think of is trying to bring death back here." Thana put everything but the note back in the box and shut it. She passed it to Lola to put away. She put the note in her green maxi dress's pocket. She knew it was getting too cold to wear it, but she loved the color of the fabric, so she'd grabbed one of her aunt's homemade shawls to pair with it.

"Thana, if you call death, the price for saving the town might be…you," Lola whispered, pale eyes wide and fearful.

Not a pleasant thought. In fact, a downright terrifying one. Thana didn't want to die.

Thana grabbed Lola's hand and squeezed it. "I know."

TWENTY-TWO

Five Years Ago

THEY GOT THE CALL LORELEI FELL AT THE LAST Thanksgiving they all spent together.

Their parents rented a large home in Utah of all places, right next to a river. There was snow all over the ground, crystal and sparkling, cold enough to make you shiver if you stood outside for more than a few minutes.

The house had ten bedrooms, 12 bathrooms, a heated pool, and hot tub. It had too many antler light fixtures and one room Morana refused to go in. She hated being stared at by all the dead animal trophies.

It was quiet and smelled of sweet wood and pumpkin pie. Her parents hired a maid for the weekend and Morana planned a huge Thanksgiving feast.

Lola and Andrew came. They'd only been married three years and were obviously still in the honeymoon phase. He doted on her and she never left his side. If she left the room, he looked uneasy until she returned.

Morana brought Trixie. They'd been dating about a year and getting serious. Their parents weren't happy, but they'd said Morana could invite someone. Mom and Dad hadn't put a rule about who. They were adorable, flitting around like two winged fairies, giggling and always touching.

Thana didn't have anyone to bring and she wasn't sad about it. She planned to put a dent in the stack of books she'd bought and never got around to reading. She also just landed her dream job on the east coast and would be moving to her new flat the week after.

It was a pleasant enough weekend. There were games. Her father was the king of charades. They played hide and seek in the dark, feeling like little girls again. At midnight, after their parents were asleep, they took rum spiked coquito and got in the hot tub and shared scary stories until Morana begged them to stop, face hidden in Trixie's shoulder.

They exchanged Christmas presents as they wouldn't be together for the holiday. Lola made them all scarves with matching hats that Andrew pinned twenty-dollar bills to.

Baskets full of baked goods like toffee, fudge and taffy came from Morana and Trixie. Thana gave everyone a novel from that year's best-seller list and their parents handed them each an envelope with 100 dollars in it.

The girls hadn't felt that at ease with their parents in years. Mom didn't mention how she was disappointed none of them followed her academic career path. Dad only mentioned once Trixie couldn't come to Christmas at the Burke's (not that anyone was going to go anyway.) Mom didn't bother Lola with questions about when the first grandchild would come. Dad didn't lecture Morana on what she could do to make the bakery more successful (stop all that hippie nonsense! Mainstream is the way to go!) Neither of them mentioned

Thana's status as a single woman and how disappointed they were she hadn't settled down yet.

In a word, the trip was: nice.

Finally, the main event arrived. Morana and Trixie cooked all day. There was a stuffed goose with homemade gravy and stuffing. Cranberry plum sauce, roasted red potatoes, and brown sugar yam casserole also made the menu. A large green salad tossed with a homemade vinaigrette and soft buttery rolls that were a Lorelei recipe also graced the gorgeous table.

The conversation was quiet, everyone enjoying the food and ambiance. Then their mother started a round of what-are-you-thankful-for.

"Morana."

"Trixie."

The two lovers shared a look, blushing.

"Lola."

"Everyone in good health."

Andrew looked a little hurt after Lola got done speaking.

"The ability to bring us all together like this!" Their father raised his glass, the pink in his cheeks showing him to be drunk.

"Our daughters and family," their mother said, in a rare moment of emotion.

"Forgotten Hills." The words slipped out before Thana could stop them. She could have said anything. Her job, her sisters, money, but no. It was the one thing sure to put a frown on their mother's face, but it was the one thing she was thankful for every year.

"Thana, really?" Mom said.

"Pie!" Morana yelled, getting up from the table, trying to break the tension.

"Yes, and apple empanadas!" Trixie agreed, standing to help.

It was then their mother's cell phone rang.

Lorelei had fallen, Forgotten Hills was empty.

———

"You're going to do what now?" Draven asked. They were sitting together on the couch in her office, watching TV. She still didn't feel comfortable bringing him upstairs, especially with Lola there. She and Morana spoke about it and agreed until Lola said it was okay, Draven and she should stick to her office. Lucky, she had a big comfy couch and a TV.

"I'm going to summon Death, or try to, and make a deal," she said again, moving her legs into a more comfortable position. Her butt was squished into the couch corner, her legs flung over Draven's lap. He'd been gently massaging her bare calves, one hand moving up her thighs, fingers under her pajama shorts when her sentence stopped him cold.

"You will not," he said. He wasn't looking at her, he faced the TV, but she could tell he wasn't focused on the show.

"I have to, and you know it. People are dying and it's my fault," she said.

"Fuck these people. Have them save themselves this time," he said, but she could tell he didn't mean it. "You're already weak. Don't think I haven't noticed. Whatever that ghost did, it's injured you. Summoning death might make it worse."

"If I don't do it, then what? I'll hang out here while they all die and then the town is empty, abandoned? They'll write stories of the spinster sisters who live in the ghost town." She was trying to make it funny, but it wasn't, not really. She stretched, wincing as her torso moved, jolting the bruises and scratches. He wasn't wrong. She was exhausted.

"Leave here. We'll pack everything up and move somewhere no one has heard of Hill City or Forgotten Hills."

"I can't do that. This is my home; this place is in my blood."

A silence stretched between them. Not awkward but feeling bereft.

"What do you want me to do?" he asked, so soft she almost missed it.

"Be with me when I do it? I don't want to be alone." She felt pathetic asking. This was new territory for her, and she was afraid.

"When do you want to do this?" he asked.

She glanced at the large wooden clock hanging above the TV. It was after eleven and all the house was dark, her sisters asleep. Only Lola knew her plans.

"Now."

"You couldn't have given me more of a warning?" he asked, finally moving toward her, hands still on top of her navy nightshirt, but moving over her stomach, her ribs, under her breasts. He pulled himself closer to her.

"I'm sorry?" She shrugged, trying to smile.

He closed his eyes for a few moments. It didn't even look like he was breathing, then his eyes opened, and he nodded. "Okay, I'm ready."

Going to the desk, she pulled out the lockbox and the hand-written note. She and Lola pored over it all afternoon until she figured out what it wanted her to do. It honestly was much simpler than she thought it would be. Draven got up and stood in the corner, near the door. As far from her as possible. She frowned at him but couldn't blame him. In the shadows she couldn't discern his expression.

"If people knew how easy it's supposed to be to summon death, they'd do it more often," she said, trying to laugh, to lighten the moment.

Draven leaned against the wall half hidden by shadows.

"Maybe it's only for your family. Maybe summoning death comes with a price many wouldn't want to pay."

"What price do you think I'll pay?" she asked, shaking as she took out the items she needed.

No answer.

She looked over to Draven and saw him watching her. She couldn't see his eyes.

"Draven?"

"I think it will be one you won't want to pay. Do you think Dabria wanted to give up her life? She died with the knowledge she left behind children. Children she would never see grow up."

"But she did it. The good of the many, she saved her baby, what was important to her," Thana argued, tucking a strand of hair behind one ear. It was loose tonight, getting in the way.

"Dabria was special."

"And I'm not?" She was hurt at his words.

"Thana, you are something beyond special and I don't want to lose you," Draven said. She still couldn't see him, and for some reason, she could tell he didn't want her to.

She couldn't tell him he wouldn't. Dabria had to die to save them all. Thana didn't want to die, but she didn't want anyone else to either. Becoming nothing, simply having her conscious wink out of existence was terrifying.

Taking a small pen knife Thana put it to her finger and dug it in. It hurt, stinging like nothing but a little cut can. She was surprised at how much force it took to pierce her skin. Blood welled and she squeezed it out from the base of her finger to the top.

"That's going to ache tomorrow." She used her blood to draw death's symbol on the top of her desk, kissed her finger and said, "Death, I summon thee." She expected it to fail. It was too simple, too easy. As she cleaned and bandaged her finger, they waited. She began to think it didn't work. She sagged against the desk, wanting two Tylenol and her bed.

"You rang?" a voice said from the couch. Thana jumped, but Draven didn't move anything but his head, to focus on the figure that appeared on the couch.

A girl, looking about fifteen, sat crossed-legged on the couch. Her hair was fiery red with eyes that matched. Her skin a healthy pink color, flushed. She wore red leather pants and a white tank top that showed her muscles rippling beneath her skin with every move. Lips covered with perfectly applied black lipstick smiled at Thana, showing white teeth with very pointed canines.

"Ummm, Death?" Thana asked, surprised to see a teenage girl.

"That works, for now," she said. Leaning back, she moved around trying to get comfortable. "Whatcha want?"

Thana squared her shoulders and looked at Draven. He stood still, silent, in the shadows, against the wall.

"I woke Dabria, I didn't mean to. I am sorry," Thana said, inclining her head.

"Dabria?" Death asked. She looked at Thana then at Draven, eyes narrowing in his direction, "Oh yeah...right."

"You don't remember her? How is that possible?" Thana asked. She felt irritation. All this time, all the hardships and obstacles and Death didn't even remember? What was the point of this if she couldn't even remember what happened or what she'd done?

"It has been a long time. Give me a minute." Death closed her eyes and she went very still.

What came out of her mouth next didn't sound like she had before, her voice deeper, more masculine.

"You were warned multiple times and still you woke her."

"I know and I am sorry. I didn't believe," Thana said.

"People are suffering here again, and it is your fault.

Dabria is angry, clinging to our night together to fuel her rage. While she was human, she understood it was simply two beings seeking comfort in one another. Her spirit has twisted it into more. Putting her to rest will be difficult."

"Why did you make her have sex with you? Wasn't taking her life enough?" Thana asked. It was a portion of the story she hated. Dabria being forced into sex to save her child.

"The story is not told correctly. I did not force her. It was not part of the deal. She offered, lonely and wanting pleasure before she died. I accepted her offer. But this doesn't matter. What matters is you should have listened to your aunt."

"I'm sorry. I am trying to make it right!" Thana exclaimed, clamping a hand over her mouth. Getting her heart rate and breathing under control she considered Death's words. She was glad her ancestor hadn't been raped. Just proof of how stories change over time.

Pain in her side radiated and she gripped the desk for support, taking in a deep soothing breath.

"I am going to have to clean up your mess, Keeper." Death's eyes stayed closed.

"I want to fix it. I'm willing to make a deal." Thana wrung her hands together.

"I know, but you will find I cannot recreate what I did with Dabria."

"Why not?" It wasn't an unhappy question. Dabria got to fuck death and then die. Thana didn't want to do either.

"Things have changed, time has passed. And obviously, it wasn't as foolproof as I thought."

Draven chuckled and Death's lip curled in a small grin.

"Draven," Thana admonished. Really, she didn't need comments from the peanut gallery at a time like this.

"Tell me the price." She sent up a silent prayer to her aunt that it be something she could give.

"You must agree to become the Keeper for all time, to prevent anything like this ever happening again."

"What does that mean?"

"I will breathe death into you, a vessel for some of my power. A vessel that will never age, never die. There will never be another Keeper from your family because the dead you will be keeping is...you."

Thana sucked in a breath, "I will be dead?" No chance at marriage, a family or doing anything that required life. Draven would run for the hills after this.

"Yes." There was a pause, but it was far from empty.

"What aren't you telling me?" She was having trouble getting enough air.

"Many things; is there something specific you want to know?"

"Can I still see my family? Do my work? Have relationships?" How would she explain her "condition" to her family? Would her parents understand? Would they think she was crazy?

"Yes."

"Will this bring back everyone who has died this time around?"

"No, the modern world has too many records for the dead to walk anew."

Draven laughed again, quietly in the dark.

"Draven please," Thana hissed. What if his behavior insulted Death?

"Do you agree?" Death asked.

Thana turned around, head in her hands. This was better, right? It would fix her screw up, put Dabria back and make sure no one else died. It was so crazy. For a moment she wished she'd never come back, but it was only a moment. Forgotten Hills was in her blood.

"Okay, when, right now?" She faced Death again, the girl's eyes were still closed.

"No, I will let you know. This isn't easy and takes a lot of power. I also want to give you some time to think. This is not a decision to make lightly."

Thana was grateful for the time. She'd have done it now if Death wanted but having more time to think would also be good.

"I don't want anyone else to die while I consider this."

"I promise no one else will die until you have made your choice."

Thana nodded, content with the answer.

Death's eyes popped open and she rolled them at the ceiling. "So dramatic. You owe me." Her voice was back to normal.

"What?" Thana asked, confused.

"Nothing. Now can I go?"

"Can I ask you two things before?"

"Obviously, you've already done so, now what?" Death looked very annoyed.

"Why are you a woman?"

"I am an immortal being. A concept brought to life. I can be whatever I want. Would you rather a manticore showed up in your office?"

Draven made a sound low in his throat and Death gave him a very pissy, teenage girl look.

"Okay, lady, what's your last question? I have things to do."

"Why Hill City, why Forgotten Hills?"

At this Death frowned, and her features softened into what Thana could swear was a pity. "Because my older brother is an asshole. And I'm a sucker for lost causes. I should have let your entire city die and be burned to the ground. That's the normal procedure, but Dabria was nice to me and I followed her home like a puppy. Hopefully, I never have to do anything like this again." Then she was gone as if she'd never been there.

"I didn't expect her to be so heartless. The way my family tells the story Death was...kind."

"I guess the one thing we all have in common is that we change." Draven pushed off from the wall.

"This is all too much. I feel..." she couldn't finish the sentence. Draven lurched toward her but wasn't in time.

Thana fell to the floor, knees hitting the ground with electric tingles of pain, relief, and anxiety fighting in her system.

Draven reached for her. "Thana, are you alright?"

"Will I ever be all right again? I wouldn't blame you if you took off and never came back. I didn't know if I wanted a future with you, Draven, but now that's for sure off the table," Thana said, tears filling her eyes. She tried to hold them back, to suck it up, but she couldn't and the warm salt water of emotions spilled from her eyes and ran down her cheeks. Sobs, huge and heavy, filled her chest and as hard as she tried, she couldn't keep them from escaping her mouth.

"I am not going anywhere," Draven said, kneeling in front of her. He held her, letting her soak his shirt.

"You have to leave. I won't get old and you will. It will be bad enough watching my sisters age and die. I don't need to watch you too," she cried.

"Thana, haven't you figured out by now I love you? I have for a very long time. I'm not leaving." He held her tighter and she wept harder.

"I love you too," she said.

"One day you will push me away and it will be my fault. But let me hold you until that time comes." He rubbed soothing circles into her back.

"Impossible." Why wouldn't the tears stop? Why did she

feel so weak, so sick? She hated crying and she wanted it to halt. She took in a deep breath trying to still the wreck inside her.

"I haven't told you everything," he whispered into her hair.

Thana straightened, her eyes red and puffy. She glared up at Draven. "Of course, you haven't. Things couldn't just be simple."

"I'm sorry," he said.

"I know."

With that, the tears ended, and she was done. She wiped her eyes with the back of her hand. Draven held out a tissue box from her desk and she noisily blew her nose.

She knew he'd been hiding something else. She hoped he would trust her with it at some point.

It didn't matter right now. She had work to do.

TWENTY-THREE

THE SUMMER AFTER, WHAT THE SISTERS CALLED "THEIR banishment" from Forgotten Hills, was awful. After spending years together, every summer, it was intolerable to be told they'd be spending the summer months apart. Of course, their parents couldn't find someplace to send all three of them, especially with the difference in their ages.

Since Morana would turn nine in September, their parents sent her to a nine-week Sleep Away Camp in Scotland. She took cooking classes, swam, dealt with many new kids mocking her birthmark and was forced to sing several annoying camp songs. She came home covered in bug bites, her skin the darkest brown it had ever been and the words, "never again" were the first thing she told their parents. Secretly she told her sisters it hadn't been all bad. She wrote letters to her bunkmate for years afterward.

Lola turned fourteen a few months before the summer began and their parents enrolled her in the summer program at an Etiquette Charm and Finishing School in London where she used her sewing abilities but had her art stifled. They refused to call her Lola. She was taught manners, poise, how to apply her makeup and do her hair. She learned to sit with her ankles crossed. Her brain was filled with information about utensils she'd never seen before and wouldn't again and how to eat without looking like a slob. She came home pink, powdered and full of proper words which ended over a BBQ dinner the very next night when she started a food fight. Their parents were disappointed. Huddled together that evening, they laughed as she told her sisters they'd think twice before sending her anywhere like that again. Years later, however, it was obvious some of the lessons stuck.

Thana would turn seventeen when the summer was over, and her parents obviously thought the time for play and fun were over as well. She went to a two-month-long college prep camp in California where it felt like she did homework for sixty days. Not a day passed where she didn't daydream of running away, up the coast and into Oregon, hitchhiking along roads surrounded by tall green trees until she reached Hill City and made Lorelei talk to her. Most kids attending with her were just as focused as the counselors and teachers on achieving their ultimate goal—going to the right college. She found herself alone a lot, as no one had time for a girl who wanted to work with the dead for a living. She wrote her sisters every day and called her parents once a week begging to come home. When she got back, she sat her parents down and they had a long talk about how future summers would go. Thana would be old enough to watch her sisters. From now on they'd leave them money, transportation and go wherever they wanted whenever they wanted.

For two summers, before Thana went off to college, they tried to recreate the feelings they missed; they planted gardens, haunted old English cemeteries, swam in abandoned creeks in the countryside and took to eating outside any chance they got. It wasn't the same, but it was something. New memories to block out the pain that came with remembering their mystical graveyard playground and true home.

The time allowed them to forget, or at least try to. Forgetting is a tricky business.

———

"Call us as soon as you get there." Thana hugged Morana. They'd talked her out of trying to a rent a car for the drive back to Portland. She was going to take Lola's beat up Toyota.

"Now remember, when this is all over you and Trixie will come visit, if for nothing else than to bring my car back," Lola said, laughing as she hugged and kissed their sister goodbye.

Morana was in jeans and an overly large shirt in dark blue that read: What Happens in the Kitchen…Doesn't Usually Stay in the Kitchen. When they'd teased her about it, she informed them it was her "driving attire."

"I know, I know. I'll call when I get there. We'll visit once you give the all clear. I have food, my cell phone is charged, and I know how to change a tire and call Triple A. Is that all, my mothers?" Morana asked, raising an eyebrow.

The little white car was empty compared to when Lola brought it to Forgotten Hills. Only two suitcases and cooler sat in the back, Morana's giant suede purse on the passenger seat.

"I wish you weren't leaving," Thana said. It was true, but she also knew things would be easier to deal with if Morana was gone. Morana's nightmares about Dabria haunting the cemetery came every night and she spooked easily. The atmosphere at Forgotten Hills was toxic and would be until Thana sealed her pact with death.

"We've postponed the re-opening. Maybe you can come back for it?" Thana asked.

"I hope so. I've already thought of five additional recipes that'd be great for it!" Morana exclaimed.

"Do you have stuff to listen to for the ride?" Lola asked. She gave Morana another hug and walked around the car giving it a once over. It got her to Forgotten Hills safely, but she was sending her baby sister out in it.

"Yes, I've got enough NPR and food podcasts downloaded for the entire trip."

"I may have added a few things," Thana said. She wiggled her eyebrows with a sly expression.

"It better not be nostalgic 90's crap," Morana said.

"Maybe…" Lola teased her.

"Or classical music."

"It's possible," Thana said, laughter bubbling up out of her. She and Lola went to stand on the porch as Morana flipped them both off and with a giant smile on her face slid into the driver's seat and shut the door.

The engine started with a rough sound but was soon purring along. She backed up, sending dust and gravel everywhere.

Lola and Thana watched her drive away. They stood, without words, until the little white car could no longer be seen.

"Are you sure we just shouldn't have told her the truth?" Thana asked, for the 1000th time.

"You know we couldn't. Morana wouldn't have believed us. She would be very upset and probably still leave," Lola said, "if not wanting us both committed."

"We could prove it's all true."

"You want to send her into the cemetery at night? That's cruel, Thana," a tinge of humor laced the sentence.

Thana turned to Lola, eyes wide. "No, I wouldn't do that. I just mean I'm sure we could find a way."

Lola's mouth pursed and her nose wrinkled. "Yeah, I

don't think so, not without endangering her. She will be happy back in Portland with Trixie and...the baby." She winced.

Thana opened her mouth to comment but Lola quickly changed the subject.

"Besides, I've eaten my weight in macaroons."

"I'm surprised you're still here." An honest sentence. Why had Lola stayed?

"It was you and me a long time before Morana came around. Besides, you'd have stayed for us. If I hadn't seen Dabria with my own two eyes I might think you need medication, but I did, and we need to fix this. All three of us put that girl back in the ground and woke her up."

They went inside. A few days before Thana had told Lola about her conversation with Death and shocked silence followed. Then Lola told her they would pack everything up and take off, maybe light the town on fire on their way out.

They both knew she couldn't do that, but it was a nice daydream...well, not the town on fire part.

"I don't want you to do this," Lola said as they climbed the stairs to the living quarters.

"So, you wanna take my place?" Thana raised her eyebrows. Lola smacked her arm.

"No, I want none of us to do it."

Thana went into her room to change. If she was going to do this thing with death, she figured looking the part might help. No stiff business woman attire, but the comfortable clothes she loved. The ones that reminded her of Lorelei.

She pulled on a violet colored cotton dress. The neckline scooped low and flowed into long sleeves. It cinched under her breasts and pooled to the ground.

"You should meet the little twit in laundry day clothes, stained and old," Lola snorted, she sat on Thana's bed, holding her knees to her chest, worrying her upper lip.

Thana could only smile. She brushed out her hair and braided it, slipping into a pair of brown slip ons.

"I should be there," Lola said.

"No. Take a sleeping pill and go to bed. You heard me earlier. You can't be there."

"A sleeping pill? It's 6 p.m.!"

"And it will get dark soon. I don't want you to see or hear this. I'll wake you in the morning." She presented herself. "So, how do I look?"

"Like a virgin sacrifice going to be slaughtered," Lola sniffled, rubbing her eyes with her hands.

"Thanks. I haven't been a virgin in two decades." Thana snorted back a laugh.

"Is Draven going with you?" Lola asked, tears in her eyes.

"No. I haven't heard from Draven since the day I got Death's letter. Why she simply couldn't just pop in and tell me, nothing like having the embodiment of death leave it tacked to the fridge."

"Well, what a guy," Lola said, sarcasm dripping from each word.

"It's better this way. I won't lie, it hurts, but I did tell him he should go," Thana said. She shook the thoughts off. She had something important to do.

"I wonder what it was he still needed to say. What he was hiding?" Lola asked.

"Who knows. Another Lorelei mystery? A girlfriend? A child? I guess this way I don't have to worry." Thana shrugged. Two days, two days with no word. He didn't respond to text messages, didn't answer her calls and didn't show up for work. He was…what was the phrase? Ghosting her. Appropriate really.

"What if this doesn't work? What if you die, for real?" Lola asked.

"Bury me next to Lorelei and then take my Rav and get the hell out and never come back," Thana suggested.

"Not funny." Lola stood up and hugged Thana so tightly it hurt.

Thana left her there, on the bed and went downstairs and through the back door into the Cemetery. The sun wasn't quite setting, but it was close. The shadows were lengthening, and fear spiraled inside Thana as she thought about the last time she was here in the night. The scratches under her dress burned and just this little walk winded her.

She followed the path, feet scraping against the ground, fingers caressing every headstone within reach. It smelled like fall, deep rich earthy aromas that made her want to curl up in the cooling grass with a book and a beer.

The gardener did a great job cutting back the intrusive vines and overgrown foliage letting the twilight beauty of Forgotten Hills shine.

The trees loomed all around her, whispering to each other in the faint breeze. She wondered what trees talked about? Environmental protection? Veggie Soap Operas?

Finally, she came to the ring. An otherworldly mist rose up around it, blocking the headstones themselves from view. It filled the cemetery with mysterious, pale gray fog. She'd never seen fog in Hill City before.

A glance at the sky told her the sun was starting to set. She didn't want to be here, but she had to be.

A figure stood in the circle's middle. Thana couldn't tell who it was. Was it Death? If so, she'd forgone her bright leather pants for something darker. Maybe whatever ritual they were doing needed more somber attire.

Thana moved closer, her pace slowing with every step, self-preservation kicking in.

"Hello?" she called out. The figure did not move.

Taking a deep breath, fists balled at her sides, she knew

she just had to do it. This was the plan. This would fix everything. "Like a band-aid," she murmured, a phrase from her childhood.

She moved into the circle and came up short.

"Draven? What are you doing here?"

TWENTY-FOUR

IT WAS DRAVEN, BUT HE LOOKED DIFFERENT. HE WAS DRESSED in a handsome black suit and his pale green eyes glowed within the mist. He looked beautiful and enchanting.

"Draven, you can't be here. Death told me to come alone." Had he climbed the wall? Didn't he think she could do this on her own? Was he trying to protect her? Where had he been for two days?

"I know. I did tell you to come alone," he said, eyes devouring her face.

"What?" She faltered and it was like her mind finally caught up with what she was seeing.

'No." She took a few steps away from him and he let her. She stumbled, catching herself on a headstone. She sat hard on top of it. The marble was cold and unforgiving on her butt.

"Thana, beloved one. Allow me to reintroduce myself." He bowed, but before he could speak again, she cut him off.

"You're…you're death? All this time? Then who was…" Shock and betrayal filled her up. She felt like she might burst with it. It was like Dani all over again, but a hundred times worse.

"My sister, but you might know her better as War," he said, straightening.

"Have you been using me this entire time? Playing with me? For what? Amusement?" she asked, disgust lacing her words. She thought about the man she'd met, his brother. If his sister was war, which one had that creep been? He'd said he had three siblings, a brother, and two sisters. Something in her mind, a cloudy hazy thought struggling to become solid. She tried to remember her mythology.

"No." He reached out a hand and she flinched away. "I would never use you."

"The Four Horsemen of the Apocalypse," she said, face blank. He flinched at the term.

"Yes, though we really hate that phrase. It's why I can be death, but why death doesn't stop just because I am here with you. I am the embodiment of a concept, of power, immortal magic, if you will, that links all things. That does not stop simply because I take a break."

"Are the four of you planning to bring about the end of the world?" she asked. She felt stupid doing so, but wasn't that what they were supposed to do?

Draven laughed, a full out belly laugh. Thana's lips thinned and her jaw clenched. Apparently, she was hilarious. It wasn't a happy thought.

"No, of course not. If it ends, so do we," Draven said.

It was too much, too confusing. Her mind was trying to refuse the reality in front of her. It was all too complicated.

"The brother I met…"

"Cessair?" He shook his head, irritation and anger on his features. "Pestilence. The man who first brought disease to Forgotten Hills and the man who brought it back when the pact broke."

"You don't get along." It wasn't a question.

"We never have. He enjoys being the white horse too much. He likes the pain illness brings to the living."

"And your…sisters?"

"You met Ailith. She does her job because she has to and spends the rest of her time with her own pursuits. She finds mortals tiresome and fascinating."

"Why did she show up as a teenage girl?" She had to know. If you had enough power to look any way you wanted, why choose that?

"What's angrier than a teenage girl who feels misunderstood, ignored and neglected? All those hormones? I can't remember the last time I saw her, and she didn't look that way."

There was one more. If Thana recalled correctly it should be Famine, starvation.

"Euna," he said, answering her unspoken question, "and famine isn't just about the need and hunger for food. It's about anything you can crave and feel starved for, like water or knowledge. I'd like you to meet Euna. She's quiet, shy, keeps to herself. She rarely appears in physical form anymore. She feels bad for people affected by her."

"I don't know if I could meet her. I don't even know if I want to see you anymore. What you've told me, it's too much, Draven. I don't understand. Why me?" she said it, but she knew she had no choice. To save her town she had to bind herself to death, to Draven.

"From the first moment I saw you, I wanted to know you, to be in your presence. At first, it was just to be your friend. It had been a long time since someone was kind to me, just because. Over the years, as I made myself grow with you, it changed. I never wanted it to come to this," Draven explained.

"That's," she swallowed, "why Lorelei was so upset. She knew you, knew you were death!"

"Yes, which is why it was my fault you and your sisters

never came back until now. I was selfish and I'm sorry. The first day I saw you, I had to talk to you. Who was this little girl so unafraid of being in the cemetery by herself? Please forgive me, Thana. I never meant to cause you pain."

Thana closed her eyes. She remembered the first time they met too. "But you did cause me pain. How can I forgive you? Your presence lost me my home. You were a millennial old being preying on me."

"No. When I made myself age at the same time as you. I lost much of myself. The selfishness was truly that of a fifteen-year-old boy, thinking he'd never get caught, that he could outsmart Lorelei."

"You can do that? Just stop being death?" she asked, incredulously.

"No, death happens whether I am around or not. As I've said, I am simply the embodiment of a concept with power over it." He came closer and sat on the headstone next to her.

"Why were you here to begin with?"

"I'm always around, in one way or another, watching to make sure Dabria didn't wake, that your family still survived. I introduced your great-grandmother to her husband, ensuring a Keeper would be born. That was a fun year."

"You play with us like toys," she said, anger flushing her face.

Before she could stop him, he reached out and grabbed her hand. "No, never that. If I could be mortal and stand next to you, I would. But I cannot. What I could do was suppress most of myself into a comparable form."

"And now?" She clenched her hand in his. She didn't know what to do.

"And now I am back to my full power and ability. That's why you haven't heard from me. It was an undertaking." He stood up, pulling her with him.

"What did you do all these years until I came back here?" Had he just been a boy wandering aimlessly around Hill City?

"When your aunt realized what I did, she took me in. I didn't lie. She sent me to college. Essentially, she raised me, best she could. I have a small home here and everything."

Jealousy prickled her skin. "She raised death, but not us."

"Yes, and again I am so sorry. As I said, it was selfish, but Thana, I do love you, believe me, please. These past two months, all the times we've met in your life. It's all real, not one moment of our time together is a lie." He looked despondent and a twinge somewhere deep in her chest gave way, a trickle of forgiveness.

"It started with a lie. You've been lying to me about who you are," she pointed out.

"I've never lied to you about who I am," he said, drawing the words out.

She thought about it, taking his words and rolling them through her mind as the sky around them darkened. He was right. She'd made assumptions, but he'd never lied.

"A lie by omission is still a lie," she said. It sounded weak even to her own ears.

"It is." He paused and closed his eyes, breathing in deep. "I wish we could speak more, but night is here. We must do this now."

He put his hands on her shoulders. She could hear murmuring filling the cemetery and underneath it a crazy wail that shivered along her spine: Dabria.

"Wait, is this why you couldn't make the same pact as Dabria? To trick me into being with you? Because you are too lonely to be without me?" She gazed up into his face, trying to rekindle her anger, but with him touching her, looking so real and intense, she couldn't.

"No. I was truthful that day in your office. I cannot recreate what I did with her. If you never want to see me

again, then when this is over, I will respect your decision."
His eyes brightened, a soft glow filling them as his hands
burned cold against her skin.

"What are you doing?" she asked. She felt light, coldness
seeping into her pores, her bones, every inch of herself.

"Do you still want to enter into this agreement, change
your life and save these people? Or would you live your life
and run from here?" he asked.

"I said I'll do it and I will." Anxiety, moths having
seizures, filled her stomach with tender nausea.

"I love you, Thana. None of that has changed. With death
infused to your being, parting from you will be torture, but I
will do it if you want me to."

Then he kissed her. Long and slow but freezing her until
she trembled. She felt her breath leave her and a moment of
panic when she realized he was killing her, sucking the life
from her body.

The kiss ended and his eyes burned black, sparkling like
crystals. Her legs gave way and he lowered her to the grass.
Eyes closed her heartbeat slowed. She began to count seconds
between each beat until she knew no additional beats were
coming.

She felt nothing. No pain, no fear, no love. She thought of
her sisters and there was no regret, no loss or hurt. Just
nothing, a void of empty. A burning sensation in her lungs the
only evidence she'd stopped breathing.

Then his hands slid behind her head and his mouth was
back on her. This kiss was hard, almost painful. She wanted to
pull away, but he kept her tightly against him. She tried to
move but her limbs wouldn't budge, to kiss him back, but she
couldn't. She could only lay still underneath the brutal kiss.

It's still Draven. Her mind whispered, trying to console
the alarm flapping inside her. He deepened the kiss, lips

pressing into her teeth. His tongue, scalding, dancing across her lower lip.

With a painful lurch, her heart started to beat, faster and faster until it moved in a rhythm just a little different than before. Her systems woke one by one. He forced power into her body, not life, this didn't feel like life force. This was something she only felt when she had her hands on a body. When she prepped the dead for the living. This wasn't life, it was something new.

This time when the kiss ended, she took in a breath instead of letting it out. Cool, secret air, oxygen fueled by the plants and trees of her cemetery coursed inside her, filling her lungs.

"Thana, it is done," Draven said, arms around her waist he helped her to stand. When he tried to let go, she wilted against him. She didn't have to look to know her injuries from Dabria were gone. She didn't feel tired or sick anymore, but to say she felt healthy wasn't right either.

"No, don't." She looked around the cemetery and saw everything like it was the first time. The colors were deeper and brighter at the same time, but the most striking difference were the people. Ghostly figures surged around them. White wisps, corporeal black and white, faded color, dozens of them.

They were silent, staring at her, then a noise started from far away. The apparitions turned, parting like a sea as a new figure appeared, rushing them quickly. Murmurs from the ghosts began, sounding angry and worried as Dabria appeared.

Like a spirit from a horror movie, stark black, white and gray, hair flying with the invisible wind. Her eyes were angry pools of black light, face a white monster with a large thin evil grin. She moved quickly in jerky half-finished motions.

What have you done! She shrieked at them. Thana

stepped away from Draven. She was no longer afraid, just full of guilt and pity. It was her fault Dabria was this way.

Dabria launched herself at Thana, but before she could reach her Draven put out a hand and the ghost stopped, hanging in midair.

You've betrayed me! Her wail sounded through the grounds.

"I have not, Dabria. Your memories are warped. I'm sorry," Draven said. He approached the ghost who twisted and turned, keening for all to hear.

"What can we do for her?" Thana asked, even her voice felt and sounded different.

"This." Draven put a hand into the specter and made a fist, pulling it back sharply. He dragged something out from the woman's chest.

A scream sounded so loud and awful, so full of hate and pain, Thana covered her ears. But that black and white evil thing stopped moving and dissipated into the air.

What remained was a corporeal ghost in full color. Dabria, looking just like she had the last time Thana saw her frozen body.

Dabria looked relieved. "Thank you, my lord," she said kneeling.

"Please, Dabria, my friend." Draven shook his head and motioned for her to stand.

"Dabria, I am so sorry," Thana rushed to say, but there was nothing in her eyes but kindness.

"I understand. You are my kin after all. I cannot say my actions would differ," Dabria said, smiling.

"Your work is done now, Dabria. You deserve to rest and to be reunited with loved ones." Draven pointed to the assembled spirits.

Without looking back, Dabria left them, and Thana could

hear her laughter as she was surrounded by ghostly family members.

"We require privacy," Draven told those that remained and the voices surrounding them halted, in the time it took to blink they were all gone.

"We require privacy?" she asked, lips upturned into a coy smile.

"Would you have me leave you now? I must know." He crossed the distance between them.

"Maybe I should make you guess," she said, periwinkle eyes glittering up at him.

"I would deserve it," he agreed. His hands cupped her face and she could feel what fueled her body now mimicked in him and it made him even more attractive.

Closing her eyes, Thana stilled, thinking. He'd hurt her, he'd angered her. She felt betrayed and lied to. But she also felt loved and cherished. Could she get past the negative feelings and relish in the fact that she did love him, had always loved him? She drew on the memories of their time together and all the words spoken between them. She considered his warnings and her stubborn mistakes.

Opening her eyes, she asked, "Was I dying, Draven? Did Dabria kill me?"

He took in a shuddering breath, "Yes, you had a few years of exhaustion and pain left and then you would die. Had you chosen not to take my deal I would have told you, but I wouldn't force you into this just to save your own life. It was your decision."

She considered his words, carefully, "And there was no other way?"

"No, if there had been, I would have taken it. But magic, it always comes with a price. Even for someone like me."

With his words, Thana knew her answer. She knew that

Draven was the person she'd always thought he was—good but complicated.

"I love you, Draven. I wondered if that would stop after my death and it hasn't. What is more fitting then a Muerticillo girl marrying death?" Resting her cheek in his palm she feathered lips against the inner skin of his hand.

"Marriage?" he asked, sucking in a breath.

"Does death get married? We can even invite your weird siblings," she said, laughing at his expression. Death's kiss freed her from so many things. She no longer felt pain about Dani or shame and misery over the Lottes. Without these things weighing on her everything was clear, sharper.

"Yes, I love you too. Nothing shall part us again." He was about to kiss her, and she assumed much more. What could be more perfect than making love, finishing this pact, in her cemetery.

But something stopped the kiss from completion.

"Thana?"

She heard a voice. All the color drained from her face and she froze. Draven looked over her shoulder and then nodded to something behind her. He dropped his hands from her face.

"We have time for that later, beloved," he whispered, kissing Thana's nose.

Thana spun around, excitement and trepidation replacing lust and love.

"Lorelei?"

TWENTY-FIVE

BIRTHDAYS IN FORGOTTEN HILLS WERE AMAZING. OF COURSE, none of them celebrated their birthday there, as none were summer born. Instead each year Lorelei picked one day, and she threw a birthday party.

If they thought the cemetery's magic and their summer home was wonderful on normal days, this day heightened everything. They were always surprised by what she had in store for them.

Whether they were indulging in the tart freshness of pink lemonade cupcakes, digging into a stacked brownie mountain, getting up early to have eggs alongside arroz con leche or making themselves sick on the castle she built from their favorite candies.

It was never a simple birthday cake with Lorelei. She created masterpieces for them; from rainbow jello cakes, forty stacked Oreos with hot chocolate that had homemade star-shaped marshmallows and Thana's favorite year when they came downstairs to find a cake that was actually a pizza. No matter what she chose, they knew it wouldn't be normal. Of course, they loved the parties their mother threw with clowns and giant sheet cakes, but this was different.

They never knew which day she would choose. They went to bed like normal and awoke to a fairy-tale. Lorelei didn't give away surprises. She was the queen of secret keeping.

One year they couldn't get out of their rooms without crawling through the blanket fort that led to the stairs, then followed yellow arrows to the cemetery where Lorelei set up a fire pit and a dozen pinata's hanging from the trees. They spent the day eating anything they could cook on a stick, fingers sticky from candy and playing card games like War.

The year Lola turned eight, they found ribbons, lace, and streamers in a million colors on everything, making the entire house look like it was covered in rainbows. In the living room an ornate box. When they looked inside all manner of costumes spilled out into their hands. Their Aunt took pictures of them in all the finery and served them tea with tiny sandwiches.

Right before Morana's third birthday, Lorelei made malted milkshakes with red and white striped straws and hamburgers. She dressed up as a character from Grease and they danced around to old music on vinyl. She gave them each a pair of cat-eye glasses, minus the lenses and the table had a checkered tablecloth.

Thana's favorite birthday was the one from their last summer. She gave them each a list and took them into town. They knocked on doors, entered shops and peered behind alleyways and under bushes. A grand scavenger hunt; their presents hidden at the end. Thana and her sisters never interacted with the people of Hill City, only polite greetings and quick chatting at Hill House and the grocery store. It was this moment where Thana knew her aunt was beloved by the town. Each person they met genuinely smiled and joked with them. Obviously, the whole town was in on the fun.

Forgotten Hills was so much more than someplace their mom sent them for the summer. It was their true home and it always would be.

———

Thana laughed as flour hit her square in the face. The entire kitchen was covered in plastic and flour. Bowls with pizza sauce, pepperoni, cheese, olives, and numerous vegetables filled the counters. As well as some nontraditional pizza toppings, siracha, pesto, mac and cheese, bbq chicken strips, alfredo sauce, basil leaves, and chorizo.

An old Italian singer crooned softly in the background, while out back a brick pizza oven was pumping out heat like crazy, aromas of tomato sauce and oregano filled the nose of every person in the house.

Over the last year, she had Dorian take a bit of property behind the house and crematory and put in a garden, a pizza oven, and a fire pit. She'd bought a fancy BBQ and some outdoor furniture. She had plans to put in a guest cottage as well.

Back behind the stairs near the pantry and laundry room was now a door that led into the new backyard. The cemetery's beauty was beheld from the entertainment space, offering cool shade and a pretty view. Its trees looming over the wall and its plants straining to get out the back gate and take over new spaces.

"I think the flour belongs on the table, not on my face," she said, laughing down at the tiny girl who grinned toothless up at her, large blue eyes shining.

"Hopefully it's a sign she'll be a chef like me," Morana said, leaning down to tweak her daughter's nose.

They were celebrating Tanda's birthday. Her neice would be one in a week, a special day for their entire family.

"She will be her own person, that's for sure." Lola ruffled the girl's dark brown curls as she lifted a tray that had two pizzas on it ready for the oven.

"Did someone really make pesto, siracha and BBQ chicken pizza?" Morana asked in disgust as she glanced at the tray.

"Why? You don't think it will taste good?" Lola asked.

"Barf, Lola," Thana agreed.

Lola just smiled and wiggled her hips as she went out the back. Trixie was manning the pizza oven, in charge of making sure nothing burned.

"I blame you for the monstrosity she's making," Morana accused, pointing a finger at Thana.

"I gladly take the responsibility for it," Thana said. She untied her apron and dropped it on the pile with the others. So much laundry, but it was worth it.

"How many pizzas did we make?" Thana asked, dusting herself off.

Morana grabbed a wet wipe and began cleaning Tanda off. "No idea, eight?"

"Well we won't starve," Thana said.

"No, we'll puke from any concoction Lola made. I think her other pizza had alfredo, mac and cheese, broccoli and olives."

"Grab the ranch from the fridge. It masks all things. I'll meet you out there," Thana said. She watched as Morana hoisted the little girl, her blue pinafore filthy and balanced her on one hip.

"Yeah, go find Draven. Maybe he's less broody."

"He's not broody," Thana said, knowing Morana was teasing her.

"I expect some lightheartedness from him at your wedding," Morana warned, right before she went outside.

Thana turned and went through the door leading to the cemetery.

The day's heat was slowly burning away and the blue sky darkening just a hair. Once she walked out into the cemetery the tightness in her chest lifted. She could feel Draven and she could feel death. She could sense each body under the ground and knew who they all were.

Her feet took her to his side without a thought. He was way in the back by the wall. He knelt in the earth, measuring tape in one hand and blueprints in the other.

He glowed, surrounded by the glory that was Forgotten Hills. He never could go back to being simply Draven and all that was death poured out of his eyes, if you looked carefully. He play acted for her family, but even Morana noticed how different he was, how different they both were. She still hadn't told anyone but Lola about her new lifestyle. It could wait until things calmed down. At least, that's what she kept telling herself.

"Hey," she said, perching next to him on a marble bench.

"Dinner ready?" he asked, not looking up from whatever he scribbled on the notebook next to the blueprints. They were planning to take out the entire back wall and expand the cemetery. She wanted to start burying the people of Hill City again. It felt right.

When Draven moved in with her, she got a happy surprise. He owned the ten acres of land right next to the cemetery and since he didn't need it anymore, he'd offered it to grow Forgotten Hills.

"Almost, you are going to join us?"

He looked up at her, those pale eyes glinting, not with life, but with death. Thana had no fear of that, no fear of him. She looked at him, constantly, seeing the end of things mirrored in her own eyes.

"Yes, I told you I would. I want them to like me," he said,

and he was serious. They both knew they couldn't spend too much time with her family. Her sisters were simply too alive. So, Thana enjoyed what time she did have.

Lola had moved into an apartment in town and was doing well. She still wasn't comfortable being away from Forgotten Hills, but she also didn't always enjoy being around Draven. Thana knew it wasn't just Draven that made her uneasy. It hurt, but it was expected. Lola worked as a seamstress and already her bright personality had acquired her a gaggle of friends and a few admirers she kept at an arm's length. She came over and ate dinner every Sunday. Her divorce was final and part of the money she'd gotten from her ex she pumped into the closest battered women's shelter.

This birthday celebration was the first time Morana had been back though. They'd been to see her many times. Lola, Thana, and Morana got together every month. Whether for lunch, shopping, coffee or just to sit and hold the baby, enjoying the silence.

"I just need to get this to Dorian," Draven said. He moved in front of her and placed his hands on her knees, taking one wrist and kissing it with affection. Then he kissed the ring on her left hand, a black tourmaline in a rose gold band, her engagement ring.

"Do it later," she said, smiling. He'd be out all night if she let him and totally ignore the fabulous pizza party she was throwing. She no longer feared to be in the cemetery at night. You've never had fun if you haven't played poker with ghosts of your dead relatives.

"Fine, you're right."

"I am always right."

"Did your parents say why they weren't coming?" he asked, moving to stand and holding out a hand to take hers.

"It's been difficult for them since we found out everything. Of course, Dad doesn't know about the whole

Dabria thing, but Mom does. She knew the family history all along. It will be a while before we can all come to terms with…well…everything." She was sad about how her parents were acting, but it didn't surprise her.

They walked toward the back gate to join the others. Draven's hand in hers a solid constant reminder that he would never leave her, that they were linked by something more powerful than love or life.

The heavy black gate screeched when they opened it, grinding against the cement, rustling the vines that were forever trying to make it their home. Thana closed it behind them with a soft metal click, shutting the dead out of sight, but not out of mind.

She'd planted grass around the cement slab that housed the new equipment, but it was only just starting to sprout. Little shoots of green coming out of deep brown loam.

Forest green and russet patio furniture clustered in one corner, a table, several chairs, and a bench. Morana sat on one thick cushion bouncing Tanda on her knee.

Across the way was the brick oven perfect for bread and pizza. In the center, a small fire pit. The large BBQ and smoker were pushed back to one side and out of the way, covered against the elements.

"Hey, you're just in time!"

Trixie stood with sweat on her face, pink cheeks, and a happy grin. She was pulling a pizza from the oven, long blond hair in a messy bun, her blue eyes glimmered with excitement. She'd practically begged Thana to work the pizza oven.

Lola assisted, bringing the finished creations to the table, next to plastic cups and paper plates.

"Ugh, Lola, that thing looks disgusting," Morana said, turning her nose up at the BBQ chicken pesto monstrosity as her sister set it down next to her.

"You never know, it might taste good," Lola said, going back for the last of the food.

Draven opened an ice chest and began handing out drinks, not saying a word. He just watched them, a bemused expression on his face. She'd have to invite his family for dinner, just to see if he changed around them. She'd been meaning to for months now, but the idea of meeting the other three horsemen in a formal and official setting? Still a little scary.

Thana went to sit beside Morana. She grabbed a slice of Lola's offending pizza. "I'm not afraid to try it. It's not like it can kill me or anything, right?" Dark laughter bubbled up out of her. Draven's eyes met hers, mimicking the dark.

"What do you think Tanda, you want part of this adventure?" She touched the little girl's chin, eyes drawn to something none of them talked about, something impossible. A blood red birthmark under her chin; a perfect Swak.

———

Don't miss out on your next favorite book!

Join the Satin Romance mailing list
www.satinromance.com/mail.html

THANK YOU FOR READING

———

Did you enjoy this book?

We invite you to leave a review at your favorite book site, such as Goodreads, Amazon, Barnes & Noble, etc.

DID YOU KNOW THAT LEAVING A REVIEW…

- Helps other readers find books they may enjoy.
- Gives you a chance to let your voice be heard.
- Gives authors recognition for their hard work.
- Doesn't have to be long. A sentence or two about why you liked the book will do.

ABOUT THE AUTHOR

Renee Lake is a mother of four from Utah. She loves bats and is passionate about women's reproductive rights. Her lame super hero power is being able to sing any song after only hearing it once. This is quite problematic when her husband listens to French pop music.

Her favorite book is Jurassic Park and her favorite movie is any version of Sense and Sensibility she can get her hands on.

She has eight books published with amazon.com, createspace and smashwords. When she's not taming her crazy kids or writing, you can find her exploring the wilds of Thedas or shopping at the Citadel.

www.thehauntedgravebooks.com
reneelake.wordpress.com

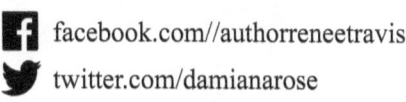

facebook.com//authorreneetravis

twitter.com/damianarose

ALSO BY RENEE LAKE

With Fire & Ice Young Adult Books
Blood Born